FALLOUT

BENSON FIRST RESPONDERS
BOOK 7

LISA PHILLIPS

eBook ISBN: 979-8-88552-190-1

Paperback ISBN: 979-8-88552-191-8

Published by Two Dogs Publishing, LLC. Idaho, USA

Cover Design by Sasha Almazan and Gene Mollica, GS Cover Design Studio, LLC

Edited by Janice Boekhoff, Lost Canyon Press Editing

Audiobook published by Recorded Books

ONE

Elyan ducked into an alley, tucked his body against the wall, and waited. All he could hear was the pounding of his own heart. The rush of each breath in his ears. Had they followed him?

Would today be the day they killed him?

His life now was a far cry from what it had been months ago. Accountant to a powerful Russian family, one of the highest paid people on their payroll. Living it up on fancy vacations, all the whiskey and women he wanted. Now he was being hunted like a dog.

The gangbangers who'd been protecting him were dead.

His mother had been slaughtered in her bathtub.

Breath shuddered through him. He was too old for this. Sooner or later, he would face his end, and it would be over. Maybe tonight. Maybe tomorrow. He wanted to drop to his knees and ask the Good Lord for more time. A second chance.

Guys like him didn't get a do-over.

Two men rounded the corner into the alley. Far too young and well-dressed to be connected. The people that had come after him were the gun-for-hire types, men with no scruples. Ones who would take money and kill a man in cold blood, leaving him leaking in an alley to meet his maker. His final judgment.

He'd be headed southward, down into the pit of hell. A man didn't do the things Elyan had done and still go to the good place after they died. No, there would be no chances for him. He'd written his own judgment a long time ago.

The young men didn't glance at him. He listened to their chatter, trying to think of a time in his life he'd ever had an inane conversation with a friend. He'd gone from school to home where he took care of his mother, then out to the club to work in the office. Even in freshman year, he'd been pegged as the numbers guy.

The Russians had foot the bill for his college education, forcing him to stay close. Taking care of his mother while he was gone.

Then came a lifetime of servitude to their crime family. Creative calculations and tax returns that hardly reflected reality.

He pushed off the wall and headed down the alley. Two steps later, he heard a noise behind him.

Before he could turn, a heavy weight slammed into Elyan's back, and he hit the asphalt. His head bounced off the ground and everything went black.

Elyan woke sometime later in a sitting position, unable to move.

He lifted his head, already groaning. He couldn't have stopped the noise coming from his throat if he tried. His hands wouldn't move. He tugged against them, able to flex his fingers, but his wrists were tied to the arm of a wooden chair.

He blinked at the room around him. Darkness stared back.

This is it. There's nothing I can do.

Time moved slowly. He didn't know how long he'd sat there with his ankles secured to the chair like his hands. No bladder control. Dirty clothes he had been wearing for a week. He could smell himself, and it wasn't good. His stomach remained empty, the half-eaten sandwich he'd found in a dumpster behind a restaurant long gone now.

At some point, the door opened, casting light into this empty room in some forgotten old house.

The man spoke to another, and minutes later, Elyan was drenched in a bucket of ice-cold water. While he gasped and spit, the man said, "That should help a little."

Elyan blew out more water. "Who are you?"

"If you think, I'm sure you can come up with something. Smart man like you. Connected." He sounded lethal. That voice coming from the shadows, could make a man think dark things about his future.

He stepped forward, and a sliver of light hit his face. So much emptiness. Looking into this man's eyes now, he could see through the window into his soul.

And it was black like oil that seeped into everything. Tainted. Corrupted.

A stain that could never be washed away.

This was the man who had been scooping up territory. Who, for months, had been killing off dealers, claiming corners, and amassing all the power in Benson. It must be him. He'd eliminated the Russians and targeted major dealers using a bomber who had been a friend.

Three of them had collaborated and destroyed a container ship decades ago.

One had gone to prison—dead now. *Jamal.*

The bomb maker had been killed months ago. *Malik.*

This man was the only one left, and no one knew his face. *Daniel.* After having plastic surgery to hide his identity, there was a single person in Benson who knew the kingpin's face... and now Elyan. Since he'd shown Elyan his face, that meant one of two things: Elyan was either about to die, or this man was going to try and recruit him.

"You think I'll work for you?" He tried to sound brave. Maybe it was better to die and get this over with. Finish it. Be done.

Find peace, somehow. Even if it was only in the knowledge that he would finally be free of this life.

"You know the man who changed my face." *Daniel* folded his arms across his chest, which emphasized just how huge he was. "Doctor George Anderson must die."

He was worried the doctor would tell the police what he looked like now?

"I can help you with that." Elyan tried to remember the man's name. "I know a guy. He takes contracts. The Russians would use him when they had enough money. He's a professional. International. He can get this done, and no one will know what happened."

"You can find me a contract killer?"

Elyan nodded. "I know how to reach him. But he dealt with one person in the Russian family, and that guy had to have a code word."

"You lie."

"No! He's so high-end there's a procedure. So that he knows you're legit."

The skin around the man's eyes flexed. "You're going to contact him for me."

TWO

The doorbell ring echoed throughout the house. Not your everyday chime. No, in a neighborhood like this, it had to make a statement.

Jasper hit the button again.

The man who answered wore an undershirt, slacks, and slippers. Doctor George Anderson was a shadow of the man he'd been just a few months ago—the head of surgery. A guy who'd been leaned on years earlier to perform plastic surgery on two men who'd been hiding from society and declared dead.

"Here to gloat?"

Jasper pulled out his badge. "Detective Hollingsworth."

"I know that you know my daughter."

Sure, Jasper's best friend Blake Reed—also a Benson PD detective—was in love with Violet Anderson. She and her father were estranged of a sort. Which happened to be his dream with his own father, but he hadn't managed to pull it off with Senator Hollingsworth to date.

Maybe next week, he would figure out how to live life on his own terms. How much longer was he going to have to wait for something to fall into his lap that changed everything? He'd been expecting it for years, but so far, nothing had happened.

Separating his private life and his personal one was impossible on a good day. He'd been given a silver spoon heritage while his friends had been brought up in all walks of life. Now they had girlfriends or wives—and they'd found religion.

Jasper had to be missing something. SWAT shifting from full-time to a collateral duty team that was on call didn't turn out to be the new direction he'd been looking for.

Maybe he should try church.

He pushed all that aside and said, "I'm not here for Violet. Or on her behalf." The chilly breeze ruffled the back of Jasper's hair, just above the collar of his wool coat. Suit. Shirt and tie. Shined shoes. "But I do need to talk to you."

The older man sighed and stepped back. His slippers made tiny whispers on the floor as he wandered away down the hall. Evidently, Jasper was being invited in.

Jasper managed to get out, "Tha—"

"You were supposed to wait for me."

He glanced back over his shoulder to see the newly minted female detective stride up the long drive to the front porch. Only an inch shorter than him, she had blonde hair pulled back and not a lot of skill in small talk. He liked her.

Jasper said, "No point both of us wasting our time if he doesn't want to talk."

Detective Samantha Jesse had passed the test and been promoted just a few weeks ago after a number of officers were killed outside what had been a fake funeral. Not the way anyone wanted promotion slots to open up. The entire department had collectively suffered a trauma during a mass shooting at the beginning of the year, and they were doing their best to move on as a team.

As a family.

She stepped into the house first. "So let's talk."

Samantha Jesse might seem new, but she'd been an officer for years in Benson, and she was shaping up to be a decent partner.

He closed the front door and followed her down the hall to the kitchen, noting the spaces on the walls where pictures used to hang. Anderson had no dining table, just a folding table and two chairs. He sat on one and put a foot on the other. On the table was a single squat glass and a nearly empty decanter.

Detective Jesse wandered over to look out the French doors at the backyard.

Jasper stuck by the island so it would seem like this was a casual chat. "Doctor Anderson—"

"Not anymore." George took a sip of his drink.

"I'm sorry about that." But the guy had performed illegal surgeries on criminals in order to hide their identities. He had a shot at a reduced sentence as it was his first offense and he'd served the community as a renowned surgeon in the years since. But that was for the judge at his upcoming trial to decide.

"Mr. Anderson, I won't waste your time." Jasper had asked Violet for some tips on talking to her father, and she'd told him to be plain and get to the point. "The reality is, you're not going to go free. But the strength of the sentence isn't completely out of your control."

He huffed. "You think I can plead my way down to

community service? My wife laughed at my lawyer when he said that. She *laughed*. I think she wants me to go to jail so she can have the house, too." He shrugged. "She already took everything else."

So that was what had happened to the furniture and decorations. The wife was only a couple of years older than Anderson's daughter, and by all accounts, they barely acknowledged each other's existence.

Jasper said, "I'm sure you can understand the wall the police department is backed up against. We need to ID the man who killed so many of our officers."

"And you think I know who it is."

"You might have only been indicted for performing plastic surgery on the bomber that was killed during that massacre, but we know there was more than one. We think you know who the other man was."

Detective Jesse turned back from the view. "Mr. Anderson, do you have any photos, paperwork, or a record of financial transactions from that time?"

The woman was all business, and he respected that. This investigation was personal to her. Samantha's partner had been killed during that massacre. Shot in front of her. He knew why she maintained absolute control over how she presented herself.

Because he did the same thing.

Loosening his grip meant things slipped through the cracks. He couldn't afford for that to happen. Not when his family's hold on stability was so tenuous. Not when he had strong feelings for a woman who'd left and gone to Africa—only to get kidnapped. She was back now, rescued by Vanguard, but after she screamed at him in the hospital to get out, he hadn't seen her.

Didn't know where she was.

Or what she was doing.

"You think I have a paper trail?" George scoffed. "The police already tore apart my life. They'd have found it."

Jasper pulled back the chair and dislodged George's foot. He sat opposite the older man. "There were two surgeries. So who is he? The police will lock the guy down the minute you tell us what he looks like."

"So he can retaliate and kill me?"

As far as Jasper could see, this man was a walking target whether he talked or not. "He knows you're probably the only person who can tell us who he is. What do you think that does for your life expectancy?"

"Guess I won't have to worry about prison, then."

"If you tell us who he is," Jasper said, "then you can get a deal that includes protective custody. You'll have a shot at doing something good and safeguarding yourself. Making your daughter proud."

George looked aside at the blank space where a cabinet had been. His career had been destroyed. His wife had taken all his belongings, except the decanter.

"Do the right thing." *For once.*

Jasper held back that last part. He didn't need to rub it in the guy's face that he'd done the wrong thing so long ago, and now it was coming back to bite him—whether he'd done it by choice or been coerced.

"I'll see what I can remember." George made a face. "My memory isn't what it used to be."

Jasper didn't like the sound of that. "And in the meantime? Can you protect yourself if this guy comes around to tie up loose ends?"

George bristled.

"We can keep you safe." Samantha kept her voice soft. "We won't let anything happen to you."

There were other options. Jasper dug a business card out of his wallet. "Or you can call Vanguard. Hire protection of your own."

A good idea, at least until George made up his mind about what he remembered.

"You think I have the liquid assets to cover what they charge?" George huffed. "All my money is going to my lawyer."

Jasper tapped two fingers on the business card. "Tell them to put it on my tab." He set another card beside it with his information on it. "Don't let this guy take what you have left. You can make something of the rest of your life. It's not over yet."

George stared at his glass.

Jasper headed to the front door, and he and Detective Jesse strode down the drive.

"You think he'll call?"

Jasper glanced over to gauge how Samantha felt before he answered. His gaze snagged on the hill in the distance and the signpost on the corner. Then, the hydrant.

He stopped.

Turned back to look up the street in the other direction.

"What is it?"

"Uh, nothing." Why did this street look familiar? It had niggled at him when he'd first shown up, but the reason he'd come here had been his top priority. Work was always the priority. It had to be. It was the only way he could feel like part of a brotherhood again. "I think I... I think I used to live on this street."

But that would mean...

Jasper rubbed the ache in his chest and set off walking toward what felt familiar. The whole area pulled at him like a thorny vine wrapped around his heart. He had to see it.

Detective Jesse stayed quiet. He almost forgot she was there.

Then he saw the fence. That spot where they used to... Yep, it was still loose. Jasper was a whole lot bigger than he'd been at eight, but he managed to get into the backyard.

Detective Jesse followed. "I'm guessing this isn't about the case."

The tree house was still there, the yard as big as a park. The back of the house had patio furniture and a huge grill, which they'd never had. The senator did *not* grill.

Jasper stared up at the tree house. "It's smaller than I remember."

She said something, but memories rang loud in his head as he climbed the ladder, so he didn't hear her.

"Come on, Jas. Dad won't be back for hours. We can play all day."

He followed Caleb up the ladder into the tree house. His little brother, just eleven months younger, needed a little help. He was still weak.

When they were inside, Caleb said, "Close the hatch."

Jasper secured it shut so the nanny wouldn't be able to get in. When he turned, Caleb had a pocketknife. "Where did you get that?"

Caleb grinned. "Let's carve our initials into the tree. Then we'll always remember being up here."

Jasper ran his thumb over the slits in the bark. The discolored spot where Jasper had pricked his finger. He cried a little, and Caleb told him not to be a baby. Needles were worse.

"Excuse me!"

He ducked out of the tree house and nearly stumbled down the ladder. Jasper pulled his badge out, and Samantha did the same. "Sorry to disturb you, ma'am."

The woman just stood there, staring at them. They used the side gate to get out and went back to where they'd parked their cars.

"You used to live there, or what?" Samantha asked.

Jasper clicked the locks on his car. "It was a long time ago."

THREE

After five weeks of working for Vanguard Private Security and Investigations, it was finally starting to feel familiar for Destiny to wake up on the top floor of the building. For her to get ready in the marble bathroom. Stand in a closet bigger than her childhood bedroom and get dressed in fancy office clothes.

She drank a smoothie while she waited for the toaster to brown her bagel, which she ate at the breakfast bar with the international news on the TV. She liked the anchor's British accent.

It was at least starting to feel comforting to pour coffee into a small thermal mug and take the elevator down to the office.

Weeks. It had been weeks.

This was normal, right? The nightmares were fewer. She didn't jump quite so much when someone came up behind her. She couldn't see the abrasions on her wrists anymore. The scar on her abdomen had healed to a red line that would always be visible against the brown of her skin.

Three... Two... One.

Destiny pasted on a smile, and the elevator doors slid open.

She strode out and caught Simon's glance. He was here more often than her, and she lived in the building. "Morning."

He didn't quite focus, his mind always working through something. "Hey, hi." He turned back to his monitor.

Since he was not much younger than her, the two of them made up a significant portion of Vanguard employees who were in their twenties. Simon and his twin brother, Peter, were tech prodigies. Where Peter had gone and trained to be a Vanguard operative, Simon had stuck here in the office with the computer network. He'd upgraded the whole thing with stronger firewalls and all kinds of jargon computer things she didn't understand.

Her desk was in front of Clare's office. After Lena had been fired for a few different things, including romantic indiscretion and other compromising sins that meant she could no longer be trusted, Clare had needed a new executive assistant.

Destiny hung her blazer on the hook on the wall behind the desk, set her purse in the bottom drawer, and didn't bother getting out her phone. She only used it for watching movies at night when she didn't want to reach for the remote.

Never mind the unread thread with her sisters and her brother.

She would only be looking for a message or a missed call from Jasper. He was the only person she wanted to hear from. Or see. But what was the point in wishing for something she couldn't have? She'd screamed at him when he tried to visit her in the hospital.

But that was weeks ago, and she had no idea how to break this stalemate.

Simon approached. She spotted the moment he slowed

his stride so that he didn't surprise her. "Destiny." Voice soft so she didn't flinch. "How are you this morning?"

Whatever he'd been doing a moment ago, he'd finished. Or hit a natural stopping point. She smiled at him, wondering how anyone wouldn't be able to tell the twins apart. They were so different.

"Hey, Sie. I'm good. How are you?" Clare had told her that withholding the truth might be part of this job. Telling everyone she was "good" rather than admitting the truth probably wasn't what Clare had meant.

"She in?" He motioned to Clare's closed office door.

"She has a doctor's appointment this morning."

Simon said, "Is everything okay?"

Someone else came over. Then, two people from the Cold Case Department.

Simon repeated her words to them.

One of the women who worked near Simon's desk in what they called the "bullpen" wandered out of the break room and came over. "Are we talking about where Clare is? 'Cause she's usually in the office by now." The woman shot Destiny a look. "When she lived upstairs, it was easier to keep track of her."

The penthouse had been vacant when Destiny moved in. Clare had married a police lieutenant and now lived fifteen minutes away in the house where they would raise their children. Things in the company had started to shift, and everyone was having to flex to accommodate the change.

Destiny hadn't even turned on her computer. "The staff meeting is still scheduled for half past eight. Clare knows that."

One of the guys said, "But what's the appointment for? Everything okay with her..." He pointed a finger at his middle and swirled it around.

Evidently, that was a reference to the baby Clare was

carrying. This company was terrible with allowing others privacy in their personal lives. "That would be none of your business."

"If she's taking time off, we need to know." He shook his head as though she should already be aware.

With the desk between them, the overbearing presence of a guy his size registered, but she fought back against the pounding in her chest. Squared her shoulders. "Clare is going to show up to work shortly. When she gets here, do you want to be found standing around, or do you want her to see you working?"

The guy huffed but headed away. The ladies trailed off as well, along with everyone else who'd gathered. To their credit, they cared about Clare's well-being. But they also leaned on her too much. It was Destiny's job to make Clare's life easier. She was running out of time to get these people to see that their boss didn't need to hold their hands in order for them to do their jobs. If they bothered her after she had this baby and interrupted a mother's time with her first newborn? Then, Destiny would have failed.

Simon chuckled. "Good job. We'll have you running this place in no time."

"Thank you." She smiled at him.

He winked. "See you at the meeting."

Only after he'd left did she think about what he said. Despite what some people thought about personal assistants being the ones who ran the show behind the scenes, she had no desire to be the boss of this place. She had zero qualifications. She just loved Clare and was fully on board with Vanguard.

After all, they'd saved her life.

She would be forever grateful to them for rescuing her from that hellish place. Shouts rang in her ears from that distant time. Under her, the chair became a dirt floor. Darkness flashed in front of her eyes. She could hear screaming, not far away.

The sound of terror. And then death.

Her computer booted, and the instant messaging program loaded with the start-up. A string of messages populated.

Back to reality. *Thank You, Lord.* He'd given her what she needed to keep from descending into the nightmare. She was getting better.

No one knew what would happen when Clare went on maternity leave and the company had a CEO with different priorities. But she wasn't going to be completely gone. In fact, Destiny had heard Clare and Gage talking about Clare being here when he was at work so she could be around some helping hands—with an assistant to guard the door when she was taking a nap. Gage liked the idea of her being safe and not alone.

The idea of a team of ex-military mercenaries having to keep their voices low because a baby was sleeping sounded like something Destiny wanted to see.

She loaded her morning report to the Famous Ones chat.

> No nightmares. The purple pj's are so soft – thnx, Ally.

> No lip gloss today. Peach eye shadow and the white shirt with the thin stripes.

She got a reply almost immediately.

> I'm sending a pair of heels. They'll look killer with your legs.

Destiny shook her head.

The girls had joked that Destiny should go on a mission with them. Or to some event where she could wear a dress and heels.

Destiny flinched. She clicked her mouse and pulled up the... "Oh, no."

"Something wrong?" Clare stood on the opposite side of the desk. She planted one hand on top and leaned over, sighing when her abdomen touched the surface. "Oof. Ah, yes. The Rammington-Harper Industries event. That is tonight. After I take a nap."

"Everything good?"

"All good." Clare touched her baby bump. "She's measuring right on track."

"That's great."

According to the calendar, Clare had only two or three weeks left. And that was how long Destiny had to teach Clare's staff to try and solve their problems without bothering her.

Her computer chimed. Clare looked at the screen and chuckled. "They're relentless. That's why they're the best."

"They really are." On both counts. The Famous Ones had found Destiny in Africa after rebels had kidnapped her and another missionary and dragged them back to a compound.

They'd rescued her.

Now, they were trying to rescue her in a different way. Like guardian angels, whose boss's name was "Charlie." And like the old TV show—and those terrible movies—they stopped at nothing to get what they wanted.

Her computer chimed again.

Would you have gone shopping?

Destiny replied,

That's not the point.

Everyone knew what the point was. They were the ones who'd coached her through recovery and how it was going to go. As if they'd all walked through the same experience as Destiny at some point in their lives, so they knew what she was going through. She couldn't push them away, arguing that they didn't understand.

Destiny wasn't sure she had it in her to make something of her life like they had. She wasn't ever going to carry a gun, kick doors down, and save lives. But she could do her part—even if it was filing and giving reports to Clare to sign.

It was a job. She had a quiet life. For now, it was exactly what she needed. Even if her younger sisters thought she should "get out more" or whatever. They didn't know what she'd been through.

They couldn't imagine.

A message from Clare popped up.

Here's the meeting packet.

Who knew when she'd prepared that? Destiny forwarded it to the whole staff that worked out of this office in Benson.

Not the entire company. There were divisions of Vanguard even she didn't know about.

Destiny sent a few emails. Did a couple of other admin tasks. Forwarded an adorable photo of Nora and Zander's toddler son with their new baby to a few people who knew them.

Clare appeared at her door. "Tomorrow, I'll show you how to prep the meeting packet. You'll be able to do it for next week."

"Okay, great." Destiny tucked her chair in and grabbed the tablet that was an extension of her desktop.

Clare had slid off her shoes to walk barefoot to the conference room. She glanced over her shoulder. "Have you thought about training...later?"

"Self-defense, yes. Sure. That's a good idea for any woman." Even if it wouldn't have made much of a difference in Africa since she'd been overpowered. "And the gun range. Though, I doubt I'll ever get a gun of my own."

Clare said, "There are plenty of weapons you could learn to use that aren't guns. And martial arts can be good exercise."

"Okay."

Clare stopped at the door. The room was already full. "Yeah?"

"I don't want to be an operative. Ever." And her boss knew why. "But I want to get some training."

Clare grinned, a look of relief on her face. "I know just who can do it."

"The Famous Ones don't operate out of Benson." They weren't a solution.

"That's not what I'm thinking. If you're really ready for this. He's got years of martial arts training. I only wish he'd accepted my job offer instead of sticking around the police department. But alas, Jasper is too loyal."

Destiny headed for a swivel chair, misjudged the landing, and nearly ended up on the floor. When she'd righted herself on the seat, Simon asked, "You good?"

"Sure." Her hands were shaking, but that wasn't the point. *Jasper?*

Clare could ask him to train her, but that didn't mean it would go anywhere. Not after she'd torn his heart out when she screamed at him in the hospital. She'd seen the look on his face, so there was no way he'd agree to this.

No matter how good it would be to see him, he had better not say yes. It would ruin her tenuous grasp on sanity.

FOUR

"You're not on duty, are you?"

Jasper glanced over at his father. "No, but soda water is fine."

"Because you're in the mood to punish yourself for some reason?" Dad looked intrigued.

Jasper had zero intention of explaining. "I like the taste of it."

The bartender set a glass for his father on the bar, and beside it, he put Jasper's drink. "Have a good night."

The senator turned and leaned his back on the bar. As though this was his kingdom to survey. Then again, his dad thought that about everywhere he was, no matter that this building belonged to Rammington-Harper.

Jasper took a sip of his soda water. "I need to ask you something."

"And I'm not going to like it, I suppose."

Jasper asked, "Has that ever stopped me?"

His father chuckled over the rim of his glass. "Before you ask, your mother wasn't feeling well. We thought it best that she stay home and not pass what she has on to someone else."

That wasn't what they needed to talk about. "I can swing by later. Or tomorrow."

His dad nodded. "Thanks."

"Did we used to live on Sierra Drive?" Jasper watched his father. The reactions were always subtle, but if you wanted the truth, you had to see past the surface. A tiny flinch. The way his hand trembled.

"Why do you ask?"

"I recognized the street, and I found the tree house where I played with Caleb."

The senator whirled around to the bar and slammed his glass down. "I'm not feeling well myself. Perhaps I have what your mother does." He left the glass on the napkin and strode across the room.

Jasper reached for his father's glass. Part of him wanted to down the rest of the liquid. But what would that serve? His mother called it a "weak constitution," though that was pretty hypocritical given she couldn't control her own issues. Anyway, he'd reminded her this wasn't the Victorian times.

Richard Hollingsworth had his own ideas about what was wrong with his wife but rarely voiced them. It didn't match his public persona as a state senator to have a wife who could use a month in rehab somewhere like the Ridgeman Center.

Who couldn't use that kind of mental and emotional reset?

Taking a sabbatical from the police department wasn't really a thing, even if he was tired and waiting for something to change.

He left his father's drink on the bar and threaded through the crowd, greeting a few people as he wove through the guests, until he reached the wall of windows.

The penthouse in the Rammington-Harper building had been designated a ballroom and entertaining space. They'd been an institution in Benson as long as the city had been here. This event was just an excuse for the company to invite their friends to a party and make deals over drinks.

Staring at the city lights stretched out in front of him, wearing a suit he only wore at events like this, Jasper ignored everyone around him. Lost in trying to remember the past. How could he get his father to admit they'd lived in that house?

But did it even matter?

It wasn't like it would change anything.

In the reflection, he spotted his father. He hadn't left. He'd only walked away from Jasper. Just like every other time he didn't want to talk about something. His father would hang around, make conversation—just so it didn't look like they were fighting—and probably get some funding promises for his next campaign.

Jasper should leave. If his dad didn't want to answer his question, things between them probably wouldn't change. He took a sip of his drink and turned. He could make a stealthy exit, and likely, no one here would care.

Clare entered the room, followed by Destiny.

Jasper sucked in a breath but hadn't swallowed yet. He coughed and tried not to dribble soda water on his tie.

He smoothed it down.

Someone clapped him on the shoulder, chuckling. "What was that about?"

He tore his eyes from Destiny and that pale ivory dress. Cleared his throat. "Nothing?"

The older man tipped his head back. "Don't kid a kidder."

"Hey, Uncle Brent." Jasper clapped him on the back, needing just one more cough. This man was his father's friend, not an actual blood relation, but Jasper had always called him that.

"So, it's not the pregnant one, I'm guessing." Brent Rammington, the company CEO, eyed the two women across the room. "The one with her? I heard Clare got a new assistant. The last one was a little...indiscreet from the sound of it."

"No kidding," Jasper said. Lena had two-timed both Simon and Peter. "Her name is Destiny Reed. She's my friend Blake's sister."

"Cop buddy?"

Jasper lifted his chin. "SWAT."

"Ah. Good man."

Something in Jasper swelled. His father had only claimed publicly—years ago—to respect Jasper's choice of career. After he'd threatened to disown him behind closed doors. After it was all a done deal anyway, and Jasper had made it all the way to being a beat cop.

At first, when he realized his son wasn't going to change his mind about the police academy, he'd tried to get Jasper to apply instead to some private security companies so he could be a white-collar guy.

Jasper didn't even make those calls. Instead, he just filled out the BPD application and told his dad after he'd been accepted.

These days, the senator was publicly supportive of his first responder son because it fit the narrative. On the other hand, he jumped in his limo at the first sign of danger and hadn't even stuck around to see if Jasper made it out of that church massacre.

"How are you doing, Uncle Brent?"

The old man wore a suit that was probably worth what Jasper had paid for his car. "Oh, you know." He waved a hand. "I'd rather talk about that lovely lady across the room."

On the far side of the crowd, the senator shook hands with

Clare, who wore a pleasant smile. From this distance, Jasper couldn't tell if Clare was being polite or if she was uncomfortable.

"She's not just nervous." Brent assessed the women. "The assistant is… It's more than nerves."

All things considered, she looked like she was dealing with the situation pretty well. "I shouldn't go rescue her." There was no way Destiny wanted him to swoop in.

Brent chuckled. "I think she might like it if you did."

Destiny had spotted him. He was too far away to see the expression on her face. His father drew her attention, shaking her hand and holding it a moment while he spoke.

"I visited her in the hospital." Jasper had waited a whole day after she got back. He'd needed to see her, if only to see for himself she was all right. "She kicked me out before I even said hello."

"Ah, so there's a reason she looks broken?"

Jasper figured Destiny would probably be horrified to know someone could tell just from looking at her, but Brent had always been astute. Jasper had learned from a young age never to let anyone know the truth of what was going on inside him.

"Aren't we all?" Seemed like the right thing to say.

"You okay, son?"

He glanced at Brent. "I remembered something about Caleb this morning."

The older man squeezed his shoulder. "Ah."

"I should go see him tomorrow."

"Yes, son. You should."

Sometimes, Brent went with him to the cemetery, and they parted ways for a while. Brent would visit his daughter's resting place, and Jasper would sit by Caleb's headstone.

Blake's father had recently been buried not far away.

So much loss.

He'd tried to find something good. Some hope or joy in a relationship or in work friendships. But SWAT had been disbanded, and they no longer worked together except on call-outs. The guys were all in relationships now, Dakota had moved to Last Chance County, and Liam worked for the Northwest Counter-Terrorism Taskforce.

"We should go out for breakfast."

Brent eyed him, finally lifting his chin. "I'd like that. I'll have my assistant send you some dates."

Between both of their schedules, it was just better to get something on a calendar a few weeks out.

Brent's second wife walked over, the one he'd married three years ago. She draped herself over his shoulder, barely looking at Jasper because she'd learned she never got a reaction. "Darling, my glass is dry."

"Good to see you." Jasper shook hands with Brent and turned away, not interested in talking to the wife. Plus, it would save Brent from having Jasper hear whatever he said to placate her.

He set his glass down and checked his phone since he already knew he was going to get in his car and drive. Usually, he was out for a few hours, clearing his head. Nothing but him, the road, and loud music. Sometimes, he was out all night.

Detective Jesse had checked in. The surveillance detail she'd volunteered for was uneventful so far.

He sent her a thumbs-up.

"Jasper."

He looked up from his phone at Clare and grinned. She opened her arms, and he gave her an easy hug, noticing Destiny right behind her. "How are you ladies tonight?" Keeping it light was better, right? Or maybe not, since the expression on Clare's face looked a whole lot like exasperation. "I was just about to head out."

Was one of them going to say something? He probably sounded like a moron.

"You're leaving?" Destiny almost looked upset. But it probably wasn't about not getting to see him.

Clare said, "Not just yet." She snagged his arm. "I have a favor to ask first." She tugged him around, surprisingly strong for a very pregnant lady. Then again, considering who she was, maybe not that surprising. "Not soon, but at some point... Destiny needs someone to train her to fight."

Jasper asked, "But is that what she wants or what you want?"

"Touché."

He glanced over his shoulder.

"We'll need some ground rules." The look on Destiny's face was fire and defiance. Why did she use it with him while this room full of people made her uncomfortable?

"We all need to feel like we can defend ourselves if necessary." Clare squeezed his arm, then spoke to the bartender. "Cranberry juice. Destiny?"

"I'm good."

Jasper lifted his brows.

"I'm not thirsty." Just a tiny twitch of the skin of her nose. Defiance looked good on her.

Except she was lying.

Not lying should be the first rule if he was going to train her. They needed to be honest with each other.

But he already knew what his number one rule was going to be.

Definitely, don't fall in love with her.

FIVE

"Yeah, girl. Just like that."

Destiny blinked. The voice in her earpiece had been telling her which way to stand for the last five minutes. So the Famous Ones could get a look at Jasper? She felt the corner of her lips curl up. She could *not* smile right now. She bit the inside of her lip. Thankfully, Jasper turned away.

Through the earpiece, she heard a satisfied noise. "Look. At. That."

Destiny sucked in a breath through her nose.

"Homegirl does not like you ogling her crush."

Destiny glanced aside, knowing full well they could see her from their positions at the edges of the room, or from some eagle's nest spot. Who knew? But they were talking about her like she couldn't hear.

"Ooh, yeah. Look at that face."

An older woman with a crazy huge necklace passed her. Destiny said, "Good evening," wishing she could tell her guardian angels to cut the chatter. That was something an operator would say, right? Except Clare had told her that tonight their weapons were words, not...actual weapons. She glanced at the line of Jasper's jacket and wondered if he had a gun. Probably, right?

"Look at her, checking out his behind."

Destiny looked away and cleared her throat.

"Hey, turn a little to the right."

Destiny rotated, angling her body to where a guy with a laptop played music, holding his headphones over one ear. Not a DJ, since it didn't take actual skill to hit play on a playlist. Also, not a live band.

"See that?" one said.

Another replied, "Yeah, got him."

"Get me a better view, homegirl. From by the windows."

Clare glanced back over her shoulder. Destiny tipped her head as though asking permission. Clare nodded.

Jasper didn't miss a thing. Hopefully, he wouldn't notice the earpiece in her ear. He glanced down at her dress, and that neutral expression ignited for a second.

Destiny spun away. *Danger, Will Robinson. Danger.*

"Oh, yeah. He totally likes you."

Destiny kept her pace easy, even though she wanted to run. "I screamed at him." She whispered the words over comms.

"Psh. He knows you were hurt." A brief pause. "Now, show me the room."

Destiny leaned her back against the glass. Cold on the bare skin of her shoulder. The dress went to her throat and cut horizontally across her back above her shoulder blades and bloused around her waist. Only her arms were bare, and the dress went to the floor. *No one can tell.* None of her scars would be visible, and she planned to never wear a bikini again. She had to give the Famous Ones credit. They'd taken care of her.

"Doing okay?"

"Fine," she managed to whisper. The two of them in the comms channel weren't the only ones here tonight.

Destiny's job was to allow the camera on the dress to give them footage of what was in front of her. The pins on either side of her hair, keeping half of it back, were also cameras—probably overkill. They'd told her they weren't taking any chances with her safety, but was she really safe anywhere? Tonight they were gathering intel on everyone here as part of their operation tonight.

As a walking camera, she wasn't supposed to run screaming from the room. She should also keep from freaking out and yelling at Jasper—or kissing him.

She couldn't tell which way it would go. After all, she was the one who'd shut him out. But it wasn't like he'd tried to talk to her again after she got out of the hospital. Or in the month since.

"Incoming."

Warned by the voice in her ear, Destiny spotted the man on approach. Close.

Jasper's father said, "You look like you might want to run out the door."

Destiny's cheeks heated. "There are a lot of people in here."

He put his back to the window beside her. "Good view. You can see all kinds of things from up here. Like how Alonzo just made a deal with Simmons." The senator pointed. "They always clink their glasses together in lieu of signing contracts. And over there." He shifted his finger to the right. "Watch Mrs. Simmons walk by Charles Markam."

Destiny watched the woman sashay past Mr. Markam. Their fingers touched, a tiny brush. *They're having an affair.*

The comms channel erupted.

"Did you see that?"

"What the heck?"

Destiny glanced at Senator Hollingsworth. "I think that goes a level above people watching." Kind of like the Famous Ones ogling Jasper.

The senator chuckled. "In my business, it pays to notice the little things."

Uh-oh. Did that mean he had seen her looking at Jasper?

Considering that, a couple of years ago, Jasper had dumped his fiancée because his family hadn't approved, that didn't bode well for her.

Destiny didn't put herself down because of where she'd come from. But given what she had gone through recently, maybe she deserved to have something good happen to her next. Was that too much to ask for? *What do you say, Lord?* Since that good thing wasn't going to be a relationship with Jasper, it might be this job. But it had been weeks, and she was still barely holding it together.

Of course, what she really wanted would never be admitted aloud.

Over comms, she heard, "On it."

After that, Destiny tuned out the operational chatter. She really was simply a personal assistant, even if Clare's line of work had some elements to it that were a little different. At least, different from a business like the one they were currently standing in.

Jasper glanced over at her, close enough she could spot the question in his eyes. She lifted her fingers but kept her hand by her side and waved him off.

"My son is a good man," the senator said. "Better than me. Though, that was never in doubt."

"I'd like to be able to say the same about my children someday." That was a diplomatic answer. She had no idea what the senator knew about her and Jasper. No one knew all of it.

It made her wonder what other secrets the police detective had.

Things he never told anyone.

"It's the hope of every parent." He turned to her. "I don't want to remind you of something you'd likely prefer to forget, but I'd also rather there wasn't a secret that amounts to a lie between us." He paused. "I'm aware of what happened to you." The senator lifted her hand and held it gently. "I'm very glad to see you safe and well, Destiny Reed."

A harsh voice said, "I thought you were leaving." Jasper's expression was pure fury.

"Turns out I had a reason to stay." He let go of Destiny's hand with a very gentle squeeze. *I'm aware of what happened to you.*

But he wasn't, was he? Not completely.

"How about we all go to Franchino's and get dessert? My treat." The senator glanced from Jasper to her.

Destiny spotted something across the room. Her cue.

She tuned back into what was being said on comms. "You'll have to excuse me. I'm sorry, I won't be able to go with you for dessert." She breezed through them, across the room. Clare had the company CEOs in conversation. She said something, and both men laughed.

Destiny used a side door, and when it didn't close, she glanced back.

Jasper was right behind her. "What did he say to you? Did he scare you?"

She shook her head and continued down the hall to the stairwell in the corner, the one that led down to the office on the floor below. "He didn't upset me." How was she supposed to explain it was a work thing? "You don't have to come with me. You can go back to the party. I'm fine."

He only stared at her. "I'm coming with you."

In her ear, she heard, "The cop is coming."

Destiny said, "I just have to check on something for Clare."

Through comms, she heard, "Shoot."

Then, "Incoming. Everyone scram."

Destiny pushed through the stairwell door and found a spiral staircase lit by wall sconces. It was carpeted so that her footsteps made no sound. Not quite the plan, but it could work.

"Care to tell me where we're going?"

Someone in her ear snickered. "Wouldn't he like to know."

Destiny only realized afterward that it was her who snorted. She cleared her throat.

"Something funny?"

Over comms, one of the girls said, "Let him go first. Tell him it was probably an accident."

Destiny stopped at the door. She waved a hand. "After you."

"So I can get suspended for trespassing?"

Destiny repeated what came over comms. "Something tells me you want to see what's behind door number one."

He shot her a look and retrieved a gun from under his left arm.

In her earpiece, she heard, "Shoulder holster. Classy."

Destiny wanted to tell them to shush. She should be nervous, out in the field. But having the Famous Ones in her ear and Jasper in front of her, she wasn't.

Jasper opened the door. He stopped short so fast that she sort of slammed into him. Then, she realized she'd grabbed his hips. *Eek.* She let go like she'd touched something hot. "Sorry."

He took her hand. "You don't ever have to apologize to me."

Someone in her ear gasped. "He's so sweet."

Except she had plenty of things to apologize for. Right now wasn't the time, though.

Destiny lifted her heels to peer over his shoulder. She got a look at the room and gasped. "What did you guys do?"

<h1 style="text-align:center">SIX</h1>

Jasper gaped at the room first, then at Destiny. He didn't know what was more astounding. Destiny smiling at whatever thought was in her head, or the fact the CEO's office was covered in spray paint. Someone had come in determined to make a statement.

And they had.

Papers were strewn everywhere. Spaces on the shelves indicated where smashed items now on the floor had been. The broken objects intermingled with a couple of knocked-over tall lamps, the shades crushed. A vase had been smashed, and the flowers lay in a puddle.

Across the wall, someone had painted an accusation that led him to believe the person who worked in this office had taken advantage of a woman at some point in the past. Except it was his uncle's office, Brent Rammington. He turned back to Destiny, holstering his weapon and pulling out his phone.

Before he dialed, he said, "Explain."

"I've signed a nondisclosure agreement." Destiny's gaze flicked to the side, and she let out a quick laugh.

He was about to ask her what was going on when she

removed an earpiece. Jasper tried to snatch it from her, but she slipped it into her pocket. "Your dress has pockets?" He gave a sharp shake of his head. "This is a Vanguard operation?"

Maybe they were here trying to find whoever had done this? Destiny somehow knew it was going to happen and led him here.

Or he'd been hoodwinked, and this was about the fact they had orchestrated this entire situation to ensure he was the one who discovered the scene.

Why else have him go first? Except that he'd *thought* it was about her letting him protect her.

Apparently, whoever was in her ear had that job.

Jasper tamped down his irritation. He didn't need to take it out on her.

"I need to call this in." Get the scene processed, talk to witnesses. She could claim she'd been with him, so he probably wouldn't be able to justify interviewing her even though she was definitely hiding something.

Destiny looked into the office, then pulled out her phone. "I'll let Clare know what happened."

He stared at her for a second, trying to reconcile the pizza grill server he'd kissed with this executive assistant in a gown, taking his breath away. He almost didn't recognize her. She'd been through a terrifying situation, been hurt, and put her life back together.

Was the woman he had known before she went to Africa still in there?

Jasper made the call to dispatch. As soon as he was done, he said, "You look amazing. I didn't get the chance to tell you earlier."

Her eyes warmed. "Thank you. Sorry this interrupted

your night. You probably weren't thinking you'd have to work the scene of a crime when you came here."

"Not exactly. Although, there was one particularly raucous night when the mayor's aide's date threw her drink at him and cut his cheek because the tumbler shattered on his glasses. There was blood everywhere and drunk people all around the room trying to help. Pulling tablecloths off tables to staunch the bleeding, and depositing dishware all over the floor."

He shook his head. "My mother climbed up on a chair and told everyone to *sit down*." He chuckled, remembering how proud he'd been that she took control of the situation. That had been a good day.

Destiny smiled and touched his arm. She was about to speak when her phone chimed. "Clare needs me back upstairs."

He wasn't quite sure what to say except, "It was good to see you."

He opened his mouth again to ask what she'd talked about with his dad, but that was way too nosy. There were a million other things he wanted to say. All of it hung in the air between them, unspoken.

Considering his life was nothing but a series of things he'd never said or things he'd never done, coupled with all the things he should have never said and should have never done...it wasn't exactly an unfamiliar feeling.

But it didn't feel comfortable, either.

At some point, he needed to quit doing the wrong thing, or nothing, and do something right.

His phone rang.

Destiny said, "I'll leave you to it," and headed back up the stairs before he could find a good reason to ask her to stay.

Detective Jesse was calling. He blew out a breath and answered. "Hey, what's up?"

"I was relieved by the night shift. Heard your call come in. I'll head over."

"Sounds good." Later, they'd need to talk about why she wanted to work overtime to keep from going home. It might be fine for now, but sooner or later, Samantha Jesse was going to crash and burn out.

Twenty minutes later, she entered the office door from the same floor, not that back stairwell. He'd circled the room twice and made some observations.

"What have we got?" She hung back by the door, leaning against the doorjamb. The hall behind her was filled with partygoers, and the uniformed officers were doing a good job keeping them back and out of this room. Sooner or later, he was going to have to talk to his uncle about all this, but that would come after they'd gone over the scene.

"You good?"

Detective Jesse said, "CI of mine didn't check in. I'm sure she's fine, though."

"The damage makes it look like someone was trying to make a statement." But it still didn't seem right. "They weren't looking for something. This is just chaos and randomness."

She glanced around. "Was it preplanned or just a crime of opportunity?"

Destiny had practically led him to it, so he was more concerned about *whose* plan it had been. "That's what I'm worried about."

"How did you stumble across it?"

He explained how he'd followed Destiny from the ballroom, mostly trying not to sound like a stalker.

"Detective Reed's sister? The one that got kidnapped in Africa?"

"Now she's the executive assistant to the CEO of Vanguard."

"I guess she found out something through all that, and they gave her a sweet gig to compensate for keeping her mouth shut."

Considering Destiny had mentioned an NDA, Jesse might not be too far off the truth. But he still didn't like that.

"What we need to know," Jasper said, "is how it relates to this incident."

"True."

"And the paper conveniently left for us to find on the desk."

"You've been holding back the punch line?"

Jasper grinned. At the desk, he scanned the transactions on the paper. "This indicates the company paid a large sum of money, in the hundreds of thousands range, to a shell corporation we know is fake and connected to this kingpin we're trying to ID."

"So, this guy that took out a hit on the whole department, who has been killing dealers and absorbing their territory, is also leaning on corporations in Benson for protection money?"

That was certainly an option. "We should go to speak to Rammington."

His uncle needed to answer uncomfortable questions about what his company was into.

Jasper walked to the door and then to the cordoned off area down the hall where the officers held people back. Everyone wanted to get a look at the scene of the crime.

Jasper just wanted to see Destiny. Even if there was a niggle at the back of his mind as to what she had gotten involved in tonight. He spotted his father. "I need to speak to Brent. Can you find him?"

His dad nodded.

Jasper turned back to the office.

Detective Jesse said, "You're different than I expected, you know."

"Good or bad different?"

"Case in point." Samantha shrugged. "I'd have pegged you for a people pleaser."

"I figure they'll make up their minds regardless. What's the point in trying to please everyone?"

"I don't know if that's sad or wise." She continued moving around the room, looking over the scene.

"I'll go talk to Rammington," Jasper said. "Find out what this is about."

"I'll go with you. After all, with your personal connection to the family, internal affairs could argue you're compromised when it comes to things like this." She motioned at the slur that had been sprayed on the wall. "And I'd like to see how he reacts to a woman."

There was a lot there they could unpack. Jasper might not care about people's opinions, but she had some loaded ideas about how he was perceived. "You think I got into this job because it makes me look good?"

She stopped at the door. "No, I don't suppose you did. Though, mostly I figure it was to tick off your old man."

Jasper said, "He wasn't the one whose attention I wanted."

SEVEN

"I'm sure it won't be long, Mr. Rammington." Destiny wasn't going to squeeze his arm, or his hand, but she smiled politely at Brent across the tiny table in the C-suite break room—which looked like a fancy airport lounge.

He took a sip of the coffee she'd made. People outside the room milled around, but she'd slid the glass door closed to cut down on the noise.

Her phone buzzed on the table, and she looked at the message.

> That was fun.

Destiny tapped a reply.

> You guys leaving?

The response was,

> When you do.

Which meant they planned to escort her back to the Vanguard building. Her permanent detail of bodyguards evidently planned to stay and "help" until they were called out on a mission. They couldn't take a hiatus forever, but they'd been in Benson since she got out of the hospital and recovered enough to start making trips out of the house. First, just to the grocery store. Then, to see her sisters at their aunt's birthday party. She'd been to see Blake, who seemed to be permanently at Lettie's Granny's house with her when he wasn't working.

Seeing them together and so happy...she loved it as much as it hurt to watch. She would never have that for herself. It was time to grieve and move on.

Focusing on work was a decent distraction, and there was plenty at Vanguard to keep her attention.

She looked over at the window and saw the senator. He slid the door open enough that he could say, "Jasper was looking for you, Brent." He glanced between them. "I'll let him know where to find you."

When Brent said nothing, Destiny offered, "Thank you."

Clare had remained upstairs in the ballroom. Gage was on his way to pick her up, and she'd be going home. Vanguard was passing this case to the police. It was just that the way they'd done it didn't sit quite right with Destiny.

Brent set his cup down, and it clinked against the saucer. "If it had to be someone, having it be Jasper is for the best."

"He'll be working the case with his partner, but Clare's assessment was correct. He cares for your reputation. He'll work to keep things quiet."

Brent cleared his throat. "Or he'll believe the accusation and take no steps to stop it from being smeared in the public arena."

Destiny would wait to see what Jasper did. Vanguard had

reviewed all the evidence and was confident Brent Rammington had been set up.

"As long as my wife doesn't discover the video. Though, she doesn't watch the news, so I suppose she'll be unlikely to find out before I get the chance to explain that it's not what everyone is going to think."

Vanguard had worked hard to get to the truth. Brent had been set up, duped far enough that whoever was blackmailing him hadn't had to fabricate much. Just enough to convince anyone inclined to believe it that he'd had an encounter with an escort. The fact he'd comprehended what was happening and left wasn't going to fit the narrative.

"It won't take him long to find the paper." The Famous Ones had jumped to take the case and hand the police the evidence that Brent had made a blackmail payoff to the kingpin who'd been terrorizing Benson the last few months. Things might seem as though they've calmed down recently, but Vanguard saw what was happening below the surface.

The kingpin wanted all the power players in Benson under his thumb. Not just criminals, but legitimate business leaders also.

How far would this man go? Would he come after the mayor, the police commissioner, and Jasper's father as well? Securing that much power would make it even more difficult to take him down.

However, that also happened to be above her pay grade and, generally, not her job. They'd all told her that recovering was her job. And taking care of Clare.

"Jasper is a good man."

Destiny leaned forward a little. "This might be only a sentiment, but don't be concerned. Give yourself a moment to let go of the worry and take a breath. Taking a second will help."

"I should have more confidence in my decisions."

She smiled slightly. "Is that what I should've told you?"

He smiled in return. "What you said was lovely. Thank you."

The door slid open again. Jasper and his partner came in, followed by Clare and Gage.

Clare said, "Gage is going to take me home, Destiny. Are you good to make your own way back?"

Destiny had the Famous Ones on hand to ensure she returned safely to the office building. "I'm good. Thank you."

She wanted to be here when the police questioned Brent. She was supposed to report back to Vanguard on how the conversation went and what they covered.

The female cop slid the door shut and came over with her hand out. "Detective Samantha Jesse."

"Destiny Reed. Nice to meet you." She didn't get up.

Jasper said, "Uncle Brent?"

"She stays." He motioned to Destiny.

She smiled sweetly at Jasper, whose eye twitched.

"Okay, then." He pulled over a chair, turned it backward, and sat astride it.

When guys did that it was hot, but sometimes, it was overused. Right now wasn't the time to be attracted to him. Though, convincing herself he was a cliché didn't work either.

He asked, "Can you explain the nature of the slur spray-painted across the wall in your office?"

"She told me her name was Honey." Brent cleared his throat. "I'm not proud of it. My wife was out of town, visiting a girlfriend in San Diego. The...incident...was captured on video and used to coerce me into keeping it quiet. Even if nothing actually happened they've managed to make it look like it did."

"You were blackmailed?" Detective Jesse asked.

"By a man I've never met, whose name I don't know."

Jasper's face twisted. "What did he want? Apart from your cooperation and your money?"

"An ongoing relationship wherein I provide favors in exchange for his continued silence." Brent held himself together. She had to give him credit for that.

"And this incident tonight? Do you think he's trying to communicate with you?"

"Who knows what he is doing?"

They'd gone over his desire to be truthful with Jasper and how he could word answers in order to not implicate Vanguard or get himself in more trouble. No one wanted to get in the way of the police department. They'd lost officers and needed to close this case themselves—legally. Vanguard had ways of doing that under the table. Or on the side. Evidently, the Famous Ones had destabilized a country once, toppling a dictator from power so the opposition could put their man in his place.

Benson wasn't exactly an empire that needed to be disrupted, but Destiny had a newfound respect for the fight. Evil couldn't win.

It had already taken enough from her.

"I'd like a copy of the tape."

Brent hesitated.

Jasper said, "You knew I would ask."

"Doesn't make it any easier."

Jasper touched the older man's shoulder. "I want you to come by the station tomorrow and make a full statement."

Brent nodded. "I would like to get away from this circus and go home."

Detective Jesse stepped back. "I'll escort you to your vehicle."

Did Detective Jesse know Jasper might want a moment

alone with her? Was he going to interrogate her? She pushed her chair back to avoid being cornered. "I should go catch my rideshare and head home."

Brent held out his hand, and she took it. "Thank you."

Destiny decided he was thanking Vanguard more than her, but the sentiment was the same.

"I'll walk you out," Jasper said to her, like it was no big deal. Could she say the same? He hit the button for the elevator. The doors closed with only them inside. "Long day?"

He was giving her an out.

"Yes, but not a bad one." She spotted something in his eyes that she wanted to ask about, but the doors slid open on the ground floor. "Do you want to go with me, get that dessert your dad mentioned? Or do you have to work?"

He'd given her a little space. But maybe it wouldn't hurt to talk with him on her terms.

He walked beside her through the expansive lobby. "There is more to do here. Rain check?"

She stopped by the door so he wouldn't think he needed to go outside with her. "That sounds good."

He reached over her shoulder and pushed the door open. "Come on. Let's go see if your rideshare is here."

A black Suburban waited at the curb.

Before she stepped outside, two women climbed out. The front passenger scanned around them. The other held the back door open. Black pants, boots, and jackets. Hair tied back and braided. Vanguard didn't hide the fact they looked like mercenaries.

Jasper asked, "This is your rideshare?"

Destiny would have to explain at some point. But did it have to be right now? "It's complicated."

He touched her hand, and she stopped, turning to him where they'd be out of earshot.

"They're taking you back to...where you live?" he asked.

She might as well tell him. "The top floor apartment in the Vanguard building."

"I've heard that place is like a fortress. I've never been inside."

Well, she wasn't about to invite him up. Not now, and probably not ever, because why wish for something that seemed so impossible?

She said, "Have a good night."

He leaned in and kissed her cheek. "I already did."

EIGHT

"Like actual bodyguards?"

Jasper sucked down the last of his coffee, which they'd grabbed from a drive-through between the precinct and this new scene. "Blake has no idea who they are, but Lettie is the Vanguard EMT now, so she's gonna ask around."

"Huh." Detective Jesse shoved her door open and climbed out.

He did the same, pocketing the keys. He'd tossed and turned all night wondering who Destiny's bodyguards were, and then wondering why he couldn't stop thinking about it. He ended up putting on a TV show and getting through several episodes. When his alarm went off this morning, his TV had been asking if he was still watching.

"I shouldn't care so much."

Detective Jesse shot him a look as they waited at the crosswalk for the green light. "Then tell me what this place is, instead. But first, I have to ask. If it turns out Brent isn't telling the truth and he got into something illegal, are you going to squash it or let justice happen?"

Jasper blinked. "No lead in? Just straight up, you ask like that?"

Samantha grinned. "It's my specialty."

"How refreshing. Usually, cops think I'm only here so wealthy people or politicians can get a favor and have me smooth out a problem for them. Like all I'm good for is doing favors for friends."

"And you think I believe that?"

So this was all to get him to trust her? She had an interesting way of going about things.

Jasper asked, "Do you?"

"If I did, I'd be reporting to internal affairs daily about you, not asking straight out what your plan is."

"Fair enough."

But her concern only highlighted his questions. Would Destiny and the people at Vanguard believe he might cover up the truth, or were they counting on justice? He didn't like being manipulated, and that's what it had felt like. The police department didn't need Vanguard's help to catch a cop killer, and depending on how Vanguard went about it, he might get mad or be grateful.

At least they weren't talking about Destiny. He was a big fan of focusing on work. After all, there was a clarity to policing that meant he could push out the personal stuff. Like everything with Brent—who was due at the PD in a couple of hours for Jasper to take his statement.

He pushed off the fatigue as they crossed the street. Parking a little bit down from the building meant they weren't blocking anyone, and they could get a look at the wider scene. Something his first training detective had taught him.

Unfortunately, a few weeks ago, his car had blown up. He and Violet had been at an apartment complex, occupied with a man in need of medical attention when a cop had offered to move the car for him. These days, Jasper regularly checked it for bombs so none of that happened again.

He had no plans to be murdered.

Then again, whoever had been killed in this building probably would've said the same just hours ago.

Now there was an officer on the front door and the ME was on their way. Homicide would be working it, but he wanted to get a look at the scene.

"Earth to Hollingsworth."

He glanced at her. "I'm here. I'm good." He rolled his shoulders.

"Then keep a lid on it while you look at the blue car across the street. About thirty feet down." She pointed at the building where they were headed, not giving anyone a clue that wasn't what they were talking about.

Jasper said, "This place is connected to the same shell corporation Brent Rammington paid off." He glanced at the car and saw someone in the driver's seat. "You think they're watching the place?"

Before he looked away, the car engine fired up, and the driver pulled out.

Detective Jesse said, "Now they know we took the building."

"Initial report was that it's a manufacturing spot."

"Somehow, I don't think you mean making furniture or something like that?"

He said, "Because I mean pressing pills."

"Okay, pretend I don't know anything about that and run it down for me."

That was an interesting way of gathering information. Rather than quizzing him about the holes in her knowledge, she'd find out what he knew about it and fill in her gaps in the process. "Gone are the days when every drug dealer has a cartel contact shipping them product from south of the border. These days, you can buy the equipment online, plus the filler to make pills. Get your base product and press your own pills. He could be cranking out thousands per hour."

"With what he confiscated from the dealers he killed, probably. He might not need to buy the raw components for a while." Jesse shook her head. "Though, how he's had no issues pulling together territory in a big sweep like this makes me wonder."

"Far as I can see, the more issues he has, the better for us. Which might account for why there's a dead guy in here."

"And who is that?"

They walked up to the officer at the door. "Who that is has yet to be determined." He lifted his chin. "Jesse. Hollingsworth."

She made the same head tilt motion. "Alvarez." Then, she looked at Jasper. "You know Romeo?"

He frowned. "Your mother named you Romeo?"

"'Cause she's got class." Alvarez grinned. "Besides, the ladies love it."

Samantha laughed. "Sure, bro."

Jasper said, "Whatever you say."

"Anyway, the interim ME is in there. Doctor Carlton is still on maternity leave."

"Got it." They stepped into the building, a warehouse with rows of dusty floors. Old metal desks, and a set of double doors, which opened up from the office to a room with a thirty-foot-high ceiling. Birds in the rafters.

He slowed a fraction, spotting two homicide detectives. As they approached the two men and the doc by the body, Jasper asked, "Didn't an EMT get stabbed in here like a year ago?"

Eric Hummet pointed at him. "Good memory. It is the

same building, and we've been watching activity here since. A confidential informant of mine said something was going down a couple of nights ago. Then last night, the neighbor called in odd noises and suspicious activity."

Lucas Westbrook straightened out of his crouch. "Which is usually someone double-crossing someone else, just to get back at their rival."

"And in this case?" Samantha asked.

Jasper followed that up with his own question. "Who would cross this guy? Not a rival. Maybe someone who found themselves working for him and doesn't like it?"

"Risky proposition." Eric winced. "This guy was tortured." He waved at a chair with cut rope on the concrete beside it.

"ID?"

Lucas shook his head. "We're waiting for prints to come back."

"Do you mind?" Eric and Lucas both shrugged, so Jasper walked around the body and took a look. "Cause of death?" He expected the ME to reference some kind of massive trauma since the body was intact.

It wasn't a total surprise when he said, "Heart attack would be my guess. There are some signs of a cardiac event."

Jasper got all the way around to see the victim's face. "I know who this is." He straightened. "We were looking for him a few months ago. He was an accountant for the Russians."

Eric said, "Before the limo bombing, after which the family just imploded."

"It makes you wonder"—Lucas glanced between each of them—"if this kingpin was pulling strings behind the scenes this whole time. Taking out the competition that was a bigger threat, the Russians, before he went after the dealers and the bangers."

"Elyan...something. I'll dig up the file and send you the case number."

"'Preciate it." Lucas held out his hand, and they shook.

Eric did the same. They chatted with Samantha for a few minutes, talking about changes in the department over the past few months. Their captain, Dennis McCauley, had been shot in the line of duty in the hospital, ironically, a few months ago and had recovered enough to come back on light duty.

Liam was liking his new job with the Northwest Counter-Terrorism Taskforce, working under Homeland Security and taking down dangerous criminals.

Blake worked with Intelligence.

SWAT had some new team members. Their sporadic call-outs were the highlight of Jasper's month.

Jasper got a lot of white-collar cases. Robberies. And assignments where he had to work with the FBI, which included Eric's wife, Stella. He tried not to show his dissatisfaction, that low-grade hum that seemed to live inside him. It might not be all about work. Part of it could be about Destiny and how powerless he'd been to help her. It could also be that he'd been offered a job by Vanguard and had turned it down out of a sense of loyalty to the police department. But if he'd taken it, he would be working with Destiny every day now.

Samantha's phone rang. "Jesse." She frowned. "Slow down. Tell me where you are. I'll come to you."

She motioned for him to go with her and headed for the door.

"Guess we're done here." He gave Eric and Lucas a two-fingered salute and followed her. Samantha had hung up before she reached the door where Alvarez watched the street.

"My CI," she said. "She needs help."

"Then let's go."

He didn't miss the surprise on her face that he didn't argue.

They had some time before Brent would be at the PD.

NINE

Destiny took the long way through the cemetery, walking the single-lane asphalt road that wound in an arc back to the exit gate. She'd asked Simon to find out where Jamal Reed was buried. She took her time. Maybe she didn't want to see it. The whole thing would seem more final.

His name chiseled into concrete.

Wind whispered through the trees, sounding almost like a running river. Few others were here at this time on a Saturday morning. Her day off. The chance to do whatever she wanted, and it was this. She wasn't under any illusions. Someone at Vanguard likely knew where she was. Probably, there was a GPS tracker on the company car she drove now.

Someone would have come with her if she asked, but she couldn't rely on bodyguards for the rest of her life.

One black town car had been parked nearby, and a woman in black pants and a long blue coat leaned against it. Light brown hair danced in the wind, but she made no attempt to subdue it.

Destiny tucked the collar of her coat closer around her neck. Close to Jamal's grave, she saw a man. Someone she knew.

Jasper's father stood in front of a grave that didn't belong to her father. He had come to visit someone? The deceased person had been honored with a marker that stood five feet tall. Senator Hollingsworth traced the marble on the front, then turned and spotted her.

She didn't move while he closed the distance between them. "Senator."

"Given that we keep meeting, you should call me Richard." He squeezed her hand.

She didn't know what to say or how to explain why she was here. She glanced over at the grave and spotted the letters of his name.

JAMAL REED.

"Ah."

The drawn-out word had a wealth of understanding contained in it. Such a small thing, and he communicated so much.

Tears burned in her eyes.

"The first time you've visited him?"

She managed to nod.

"And you're not here to spit on his grave, or scream something you don't want me to hear?"

She glanced over.

He shrugged. "We all grieve in our own way."

"No." She cleared her throat. "I won't be doing either of those things."

"Good." He held his elbow out. "Allow me to escort you."

As she slid her arm through his and they walked to Jamal's grave, the last thing she wanted was to assume the worst about this gentleman. It was easier to dislike someone and close herself off, to protect herself from any harm that might come. Sounded proactive—or like she had healthy boundaries.

Instead, she would only be acting unfairly.

They stood side by side in front of Jamal's grave.

"He died while you were in Africa. Isn't that right?"

"Yes." She had to clear her throat again. "He was my father."

Richard tensed. She let go of his elbow, feeling the need to stand on her own two feet, and stared at the headstone. The dates.

"No one knows but me." The wind ruffled her collar against her cheek. "My mother was drunk one night, jealous of my relationship with my little sisters, I guess. I'd put them all to bed. Blake was working at the gas station. He was in college, too, so he'd take his homework with him for when it was quiet overnight. She took great pleasure in telling me I was the result of a conjugal visit not long after he was convicted."

It hadn't made her feel any differently about her sisters. Much to her mother's dismay, the attempt to drive a wedge between Destiny and Grace, Mercy, and Hope hadn't worked. They were still blood, even if only her half-sisters. The news made Blake her full brother. Something he probably didn't know even now.

And would he care?

Blake had adopted all of them, and they'd changed their last names to his despite auntie and uncle nay-sayers. He just wanted them to be a family.

"None of us is entirely the sum of where we came from. We're more than that. Or less, in some cases." Richard fell silent for a second. "You are who you want to be, Destiny. Who the Good Lord made you to be."

"I didn't get to say goodbye."

The massacre had occurred while she was en route home from Africa.

"I also cost myself the chance to say goodbye." He cleared his throat.

She could see the name on the marker across the way. So close to her father's final resting place.

Richard said, "My son died, and I was not there. It is my greatest regret."

"I'm sorry." It sounded so lame. "I didn't know you had lost a child."

"Jasper's brother, Caleb." Richard's tone thickened. "He had leukemia."

A tear rolled down her face.

"I know where he is." Richard looked at the sky. "He's not here. And the same can be said of your father, can't it?"

"He believed." Her father's faith had been strong. "But he also did a lot of bad things."

"Forgiveness is the only hope I have. The thing I cling to when I have nothing." Richard sniffed, and it had nothing to do with the chill in the air. "I pretended to forget. It's helped, but I realized I've lost so much."

She'd tried to forget what happened to her in Africa. Maybe that was okay for a while, but she shouldn't push it away forever. Everyone said she had to "work through it," and this man proved that forgoing that step might not be a good long-term solution.

Richard turned to the headstone. "I heard he turned his life around in prison."

Hearing that brought a smile to her face.

"What is it?"

"I'm the one who shared with him. I told him what God had done for me." It seemed so long ago now. So much had changed—she almost felt like a completely different person these days. Jasper practically didn't recognize her; he'd kept looking at her like she was a stranger.

What should she make of it?

Should she reinvent herself or get back to who she had been? She hadn't even gone to her townhouse, but instead, she had Vanguard clear out her things and put them in storage so the landlord could rent it out to someone else.

She didn't fit in her old life. That girl seemed far too naïve now, and if she lived that life, she would be vulnerable, in danger. When those men had driven into the compound and grabbed her...

Destiny hadn't known what to do. She hadn't been able to save Isadora.

She wanted to be able to fight back, but was she strong enough to get there? It would be easier to hide in the penthouse, do her job, and never need to be that person. Keep the danger out of her life. But she couldn't closet herself away forever.

"Maybe one day, you could tell me the story. I'd like to hear it." Richard glanced toward the car.

"Another time, absolutely." She didn't want to keep him from the woman waiting for him. His wife? She had never met Jasper's mother and didn't know much about her. No one really did.

"Thank you, Ms. Reed."

She didn't ask him to call her Destiny. The respect of him saying her name that way was something she appreciated. "You're welcome."

He started to turn away. "I'll leave you to your—"

His body jerked, and he grunted. Started to go down. Destiny grabbed his arm, and he cried out.

She let go, and he fell to his knees on the grass. Blood on his sleeve. "What happened?"

He gasped. "I think I've been shot."

She looked around, trying to find some kind of cover in case whoever fired that bullet tried again. Over by the car, the woman now lay on the ground.

"Look!" She pointed.

"Elaine!" He started to get up.

"We need to stay low." She pulled out her phone, her hand shaking. The rumble of Jeep tires on dirt swelled in her mind. She could feel the heat of the African sun and smell the tang of gunfire. "Stay low."

Destiny turned the phone in her hand and swiped her hand up the screen, then dialed one.

"Vanguard."

"Four seven two." Her designation plus the "shots fired" code they'd made her memorize even though she'd argued she wasn't going to be in danger.

"Copy that." Whoever was on call said, "Do you have cover?"

"No, and there are multiple victims." Destiny gasped. Why was her skin flushed? "I need an ambulance and help."

"Sniper?"

"I don't know!" Destiny raced low behind the senator over to his car. Another bullet pinged off a headstone beside her. She stumbled, twisting her ankle in the grass. Her phone went flying. "We're being shot at!"

Richard turned, crouched by the woman. "My wife has been shot!"

Destiny needed to curl into a ball. Wrap her arms around her middle and squeeze her eyes shut. Pretend this wasn't happening.

But it hadn't worked last time. It hadn't changed a thing.

Nothing had.

Instead, she pulled off her coat and crawled to the senator, pressing the fabric against the wound. The woman on the ground stared up at her with hatred in her gray eyes. "I won't let you kill me."

She scratched her nails down Destiny's face.

TEN

"April, we need you to tell us what happened." Detective Jesse leaned her hip against the side of the hospital bed.

The girl had been admitted and treated for injuries consistent with being beaten. She brushed hair off her cheek with a shaky hand. Two of her fingers had been taped together. She had a bandage on the side of her head, and her ribs had been wrapped.

Jasper hung back by the doorway of the emergency bay so he didn't intimidate her, just in case this was about an attack by a stranger, and his proximity affected her willingness to talk.

Samantha's CI was maybe nineteen. Slender, but not like she didn't eat, with long dark hair that had some streaks of different colors in it. He'd listened to his mom talk about bad hair dye jobs often enough that he knew more than he wanted to.

April sniffed. "I can't stay here. He'll find me, and it'll start all over again."

"Who did this to you? Neal?" Samantha shifted, her body language irritated.

She'd told him on their way to get April that Neal was April's ex-boyfriend. She also had a father who'd raised her, but by all accounts, he was pretty much absent.

"He didn't mean it. He's under a lot of pressure."

"But you think it'll happen again?" Samantha asked softly.

Jasper had zero tolerance for a guy who beat on his girlfriend. He'd seen the worst outcomes of a relationship like that—if you could even call it a relationship—too many times to not want to step in when the early warning signs were there. Or in a situation like this, where April believed the outcome would be inevitable.

His phone started to ring in his pocket, thankfully on silent. "There are places you can go where you can be safe."

She shook her head. "He'll find me." Her voice dropped. "He said he'll kill me if he sees me again."

"We can keep you safe."

"His friends are after me, too. They think I know where he hid the stash, and they're going to come looking." April's eyes filled with tears. "They're going to kill me because I don't know where he hid it."

"What does he have?"

"Two hundred thousand dollars." April whimpered. "I told him we should go somewhere, disappear. Like a beach. We don't have to stay here."

And then he'd beaten her because her idea didn't fit his plan—or simply because she thought of it first. If she dinged his pride, a guy like that would lash out.

"He said he'd be back. I think he was going to use me to get the jump on them when they came looking for him. He'd have let them kill me."

Samantha laid her hand on April's arm. "We're not going to let that happen. There are safe houses. You don't have to go to a shelter. We can keep you protected."

"I can't go to a motel. Someone will see me."

Jasper's phone rang again. He pulled it out and saw Gage's number, along with two missed calls from the lieutenant. "I need to take this."

"Sure thing."

Since Samantha was good, he stepped out of the bay. Just then, the doors to the emergency entrance swung open, and EMTs pushed a woman on a gurney with two people running behind them.

Jasper's mind blanked. His entire body stilled.

Mom?

His dad ran behind the bed, holding something on his arm. Destiny had blood running down her cheek.

"Watch out." The EMTs passed him. His mom was pale. Eyes glassy. She had bandages on her shoulder, all piled up, the other EMT holding pressure on it as they moved.

Recognition registered on his mom's face. "Jasper! She tried to kill me, Jasper!"

He didn't move. His dad stopped beside him, and Jasper felt his father's grip on the side of his neck. "I've got this. You help Destiny."

Two nurses and a doctor had followed Jasper's mom. He could hear the commotion; his mom still yelling about someone trying to murder her.

"Take care of her." Jasper's dad gave his neck a squeeze and let go.

A nurse said, "Senator. Let's get that arm looked at."

Jasper turned to Destiny. "What happened?" She was hurt. "Let's get someone to look at your cheek." He took her hand and tugged her to the desk. "This woman needs to see someone."

"She can sit down. We need some information first." The nurse handed a clipboard over. "We just had a couple of emergencies come in, so we're busy right now. Take a seat, and we'll get to you."

Jasper's stomach clenched. "She's bleeding."

The nurse went to a cabinet and handed over a bandage. "Hold this on it. We'll get to you." She sat back down and looked at her computer screen.

Jasper started to argue. Destiny tugged him to the waiting area where she sank into a seat. He crouched in front of her, ignoring the people around them. Injuries and sickness. He didn't want Destiny near any of this. He took the bandage and held it against her cheek. "What happened?"

She sucked in a breath. Closed her eyes for a second. "Your father was grazed. The bullet hit your mother."

"And the shooter?"

"The police that showed up started to search for whoever it was. I never saw them." She bit her lip. "They think I did it and tossed the gun in a bush. Your dad told them that's not what happened, so they didn't just arrest me. But they had the cuffs out and everything. They think I tried to kill your parents."

He shook his head. "That's ridiculous. Nothing is going to happen, and no one is going to arrest you."

"You should go see your mother. You should be with your dad." She shifted in the seat, squaring her shoulders like she needed to be strong on her own. "They need you."

"My dad told me to stay with you."

She frowned. "Why would he say that?"

"Because he's a good guy. He has a lot on his shoulders, but he has his priorities straight."

"But Tessa..."

Why was this coming up now, of all times? "There was a lot Tessa didn't understand. She wasn't privy to all of it."

"You were engaged."

Jasper wasn't afraid of the truth. "Yes, we were." And after they broke up, Destiny showed up at his house drunk and kissed him. He'd never understand women, but one day, he'd ask her why she did that. "We don't need to talk about this now. You aren't being arrested because no one thinks you tried to shoot my parents."

"I don't even have a gun."

"There you go." He shifted the bandage off her cheek. "The bleeding has slowed. Were you grazed by the bullet?" That wasn't what this looked like.

"Your mom scratched me."

Jasper's stomach clenched. "Sorry."

What was he supposed to say? He and Dad had been covering for her for years. He just hadn't thought he'd have to do it with Destiny. He'd hoped to introduce them on a good day. A pipe dream at best, considering the alternative was to keep them apart. If the relationship with Destiny amounted to something long term—which he could admit was what he wanted—would he really separate himself from his family just so she didn't have to deal with it?

And now that she had a glimpse, it was going to be even harder to keep everything straight.

He had to lock this thing down.

If that meant nothing ever happened between him and Destiny, then so be it. That might be the best outcome for everyone.

She stared at him with her lips parted. Of course there were things she wanted to say, but a nurse showed up and took her to a bay. Jasper checked back with Samantha and

April. Then, he found his father in a bay of his own, getting his arm stitched up by one doctor while another stood on the other side of the bed.

"She's sedated now," the other doctor said, "and we will take care of the gunshot wound. The police will want a full statement."

His father looked older than Jasper had ever seen him look, his face pale.

"Senator, has your wife..." He cleared his throat. "Has she ever received psychiatric care?"

Jasper turned and walked down the hall, not wanting to stick around and hear what his dad said. It would be harder for both of them that way.

He spotted Destiny. A nurse wiped something gel-like on her cheek. Probably to keep her from getting an infection. *Your mom scratched me.* He ran a hand over the front of his shirt, the left side of his abdomen.

Why do you have to be like this?

His question had been ignored, his mom too far gone to even comprehend what was happening—or what she had done.

Jasper had to choose between his parents, his job, and Destiny.

One choice might lead to happiness. The other was his duty.

How on earth was he going to choose?

ELEVEN

The screen of Destiny's phone flashed with two letters: *FO*.

Finally. She swiped and put the phone to her cheek. "Where were you guys?" Her thumb bumped the scratch on her cheek. *Ouch*.

"We lost him." To her credit, she sounded mad. The Famous Ones weren't happy.

"Who?"

"The shooter."

Destiny scooted to the edge of the bed and slid her feet into her shoes. She'd had the scratch cleaned and bandaged. Time to see how Richard and his wife were doing. Especially if she wasn't going to be arrested.

Could she go home, crawl into bed, and forget this day ever happened?

That sounded good.

But first... "You went after the shooter?"

"Of course, we did. He shot at you!" They had her on speaker. And as per usual, their voices blended together until she couldn't tell which one was speaking. Or her head was swimming, and she needed to lie down. Probably both.

One of the others said, "He could've killed you. He nearly killed that woman."

"She's Jasper's mother," Destiny said.

Someone gasped.

"And I'm about to go see how she is."

"Call us back. We wanna know."

Destiny said, "I need to get back to Vanguard. But if you guys are busy—"

"We'll split up." There was a pause. "Ten minutes."

"Copy that." Destiny hung up, too exhausted to figure out how better to sign off the call. They had been there, saw what happened, and then jumped on a pursuit. Leaving her to think she was alone with Jasper's parents. Facing the police who had taken his mother's word that she had been the shooter.

She couldn't even process how nuts that was.

Why would Mrs. Hollingsworth say that? Jasper hadn't seemed surprised when she'd told him. Another confusing part of this. She needed a nap to be able to start to process it.

Destiny filled out the paperwork to get checked out.

Her phone rang. Her brother was calling her. She silenced it and headed for the Hollingsworths' rooms. Maybe Jasper's mom was in surgery or something. She spotted Detective Jesse in a bay talking with a young woman and Jasper. It looked serious. Two officers stood in the hall.

She approached them. "Is Senator Hollingsworth around here? Or his wife?"

One lifted his chin. "Who are you?"

His suspicious look rubbed her the wrong way. She didn't know these guys, and they didn't know her. "Destiny Reed. I work for Vanguard."

"And you fit the description the victim gave us of her shooter."

Destiny took a step back.

"Hey, guys. What's going on?"

She whirled to find her brother and Violet walking down the hall. Blake had his badge on his belt and an unhappy look on his face.

"Wait," the officer said. "Is this one of your sisters?"

Violet pulled Destiny into a hug. "We should get you out of here."

She glanced at Blake, who was speaking with the two officers, and then she went with Violet down the hall. Back to where she could see Jasper. "I need to go home."

"Yes, you do." Violet wrapped her fingers around Destiny's wrist.

She looked at the tight placement of her fingers. Her brother's girlfriend—fiancée, whatever they were—was feeling for her pulse. Her heart rate. "Did Clare send you?"

"She called. We were already on our way."

Blake turned away from the officers and came over. "You didn't answer your phone."

Tears gathered in her eyes.

His expression softened, and he pulled her into a hug. She ended up sandwiched between the two of them, fighting back tears. Until she realized she was safe enough here. She didn't need to fight. They let her cry for a few minutes.

When Blake eased back, Violet didn't let go of her.

He said, "Let's take you home."

Violet's phone beeped. She glanced at the screen. "We're swiping in the two detectives and their witness. She needs protection, and Vanguard is going to provide it."

Jasper stepped out of their bay. "You heard?"

He barely looked at Destiny, more like just glanced through her.

It was Violet who said, "Yes. You'll follow us?"

"Will do." He held the door for Detective Jesse and the witness.

Detective Jesse frowned and asked, "You really aren't going to stay with your parents?"

Jasper closed the sliding door behind the scared-looking girl. She had a jacket on over the hospital gown, and her clothes were in a bag tucked close to her front.

He said, "I'll drop you guys and come back. They aren't going anywhere."

Blake glanced at Destiny, his expression inscrutable.

"Let's go." Violet put her arm around Destiny.

She needed to be alone, somewhere quiet where she felt safe. Somewhere she didn't have to put on a brave face and try to explain that she hadn't been in possession of a weapon, hadn't been the one who shot the senator and his wife, and didn't know why that woman had accused her of it.

Was Jasper going to settle the issue for her?

Along with not seeming all that surprised, he also hadn't offered her a reason why his mom might do that. Maybe he had no idea. Or maybe it was exactly the kind of thing she did.

He walked ahead of her, with the witness Vanguard would be protecting and his colleague. Since he'd come out of the room, he'd barely looked at her. So much for spending time with him, hearing stories about his brother who'd died. Getting to know the sibling Jasper had loved and lost.

Violet tucked her into the front seat of Blake's truck. Destiny leaned her head on her hand and closed her eyes, trying not to think about how much her cheek stung. Whoever that girl was, her deal was more important. Police business was more important. Saving lives took priority over answering her questions.

Kind of like how taking a nap should take priority rather than overthinking this thing to death. She'd yelled at Jasper, he hadn't come around again...and now this. The last couple of days were more confusing than she could worry about.

Blake pulled up out front, and she jerked her eyes open.

Destiny stared up at the Vanguard building. "What am I even doing here?"

"You said this is where you wanted to be."

Violet said, "I don't think that's what she means."

Blake shifted in his seat. "Well, then, what does she mean?"

"I have no qualifications. I'm a waitress." She twisted in her seat so she could see both of them. "I'm a victim. I'm not qualified to be an executive assistant!"

Blake glanced out the back window. Jasper's vehicle must have pulled up behind them.

Violet said, "Clare wouldn't have hired you if she didn't think you could do it. And it's natural to have self-doubts."

Destiny pushed out a long sigh. Neither of them understood, and she couldn't explain it.

Blake winced. "I'll send the girls over. You'll feel better when you've hung out with them."

She shook her head, which made her cheek sting again. "Maybe another day."

"It's not good to hide away and wallow."

"I like the quiet."

"You need people around you who support you and love you."

"Who decided that?" That wasn't some general rule. "Maybe I want to be alone because I like it. I need to *think*. I can't do that in a room full of people."

"You want to sulk."

Destiny twisted around, shoved the door open, and stumbled out. That was really what he thought?

Jasper reached for her, but she stepped out of reach.

"I don't need help."

Violet could show them upstairs. After all, she had the information for what was going on. Destiny had nothing, but everyone seemed to have an opinion on what she should do about it.

Her shoes echoed on the lobby tile. They'd have to use the normal elevator. She said hi to Susan behind the reception desk and swiped her card to enter the hall behind the desk. At the end, she used her code to call the private elevator that only stopped at Clare's office and the penthouse.

When the doors opened on the top floor, the entryway was full of women. Allyson put her hand on her hip. "You were supposed to wait for us."

Destiny burst into tears.

"DEFCON 1." Allyson tugged her into the apartment and over to the couch. "This woman needs ice cream, stat."

Destiny slumped onto the couch and pulled a pillow over her face so she could cry without anyone seeing.

She was supposed to be better now. She was supposed to have survived, to be strong. No one was supposed to accuse her of trying to kill them. She should've been able to say goodbye to her father. Her brother should understand. He should have realized she was his full sister and nothing like the girls. Jasper should've mentioned he had a brother who died.

Someone should've noticed she was pregnant.

TWELVE

Simon Olson generally stuck to the office, but today, he was on the street wearing a suit that didn't fit right. "Yes, your security footage. I'm wondering if you have a view of that gate over there."

The bank manager frowned. "The one for the cemetery?"

"That's right." Simon nodded.

"We heard there was a shooting over there. Are you with the police?"

"I work for Vanguard."

"Ah." He turned to the front entrance, and the automatic doors slid open. "You must be working with the police on this one. I'll go fetch a copy."

Simon followed him in. "You don't need to transfer it to a flash drive or anything." Most non-techy people didn't even know how to do that.

"It's all backed up to the cloud. Do you want me to email it to you?" The manager walked down a hallway and stopped at a cubicle close by, where a young woman typed on her computer. "Julie, honey, can you help this Vanguard agent get what he needs?"

"Yes, sir." She smiled politely at her boss.

Simon explained succinctly what he needed from her, and she accessed the online portal for their surveillance like an employee who knew what she was doing—not always a given.

The interplay between her and her boss was *not* something he needed to get into. Whoever these people were, they weren't stuck. They had a choice to stay or to leave. They were free to make whatever decisions they wanted.

Simon fought for people in situations where their choices had been stripped from them.

People like Destiny, who'd tried to do a good thing, and it had gone horrifyingly wrong. Like his mother, who had testified against his father's criminal activities, and he'd murdered her for it. And so many more of his friends.

He might do it online and not with a gun or kicking down doors or punching people. But he fought in his own way.

Like trying to identify who had shot at Destiny just a few hours ago and nearly killed someone. The latest report was that Jasper's mom was stitched up but hadn't been released yet. Or like finding the person who had been using a program *he* wrote to help a criminal kingpin stay under the radar.

Everyone was trying to find this guy.

Simon, too, but for an entirely different reason. If he could find the kingpin, then he would discover who had stolen his code and used it to further their criminal activity. Sure, he'd written it back when he hadn't been on the straight and narrow. But he and his twin had turned their lives around—thanks to Clare.

"Here you go." She brought up the dashboard and all their camera feeds.

He tapped her screen. "This one."

She clicked it.

He said, "Two hours ago, maybe a bit less. We're looking for someone leaving."

"This is very exciting. Are you on a *case?*"

"Someone nearly died this morning," he said. "I wouldn't call that exciting."

She shut down. He might've said that with a tone, but his bad relationship with Lena started with her being entirely too interested in what he did. She'd managed to make him feel special.

Apparently, she'd also been making his brother feel special at the same time.

He liked Destiny a whole lot better and had zero romantic feelings for her. He could care and not get distracted from work.

On the screen, a car pulled out of the cemetery fast. The rear entrance was only used by maintenance personnel, and they had golf carts they drove around in. No one would've pulled a car in there.

I need that license plate.

Aloud, he said, "Can you send me that footage?"

"Uh." She moved the mouse but didn't seem to know where to go.

"May I?"

She slid her chair back.

Simon tapped keys, inputting a command that would connect the WiFi to his VPN at Vanguard. The screen went black, and green text scrolled. He put in several more commands.

"Is it supposed to do that?"

He tapped the last line and hit enter. The screen reverted to the web browser she'd had up, and he sent the file to himself. Then, he disconnected it all from his system and made her machine forget anything happened.

Too bad he couldn't do that with all his bad memories. And mistakes.

"Done." He straightened. "Thanks for your help."

"Uh...you're welcome?"

He strode out of the bank and into the bright sun and the chilly breeze. The winter weather suited him best. Heat only reminded him of growing up in Malaysia. Peter had moved on and "found God" for real. Like they hadn't found Him as kids? Simon had learned painful lessons on what God was like.

Peter thought he should travel a similar path. But no. Going back to God would feel far too much like revisiting the worst time in his life.

Not. Gonna. Happen.

He checked the footage on the tablet he had in his car, using a program he'd written to add clarity to a grainy picture. The same program that had allowed the Famous Ones to find Destiny and rescue her. Just not before the worst had happened.

He had to push it aside, though. He couldn't change the past. All he could do was work to make the best future possible. For everyone.

No one could ask more than that.

Not even the Almighty.

THIRTEEN

It was past six in the evening by the time Jasper headed up the elevator inside Vanguard, this time to the penthouse. He'd helped Samantha get April settled in the tiny apartment a couple of floors below.

He'd called Destiny more than once, but she hadn't answered. Hopefully, she'd rested. He texted her, asking if he could come and see her, and she'd had Susan at the reception desk provide him with a card to get all the way to the top floor.

At least she lived in a place that was secure.

When someone had been after Roxie, they'd targeted her house. The one she shared with Destiny. He'd helped protect both of them. Then, when she was in Africa...

He had tried not to be a stalker, but she hadn't messaged him back in a few days. He'd gone to Simon and asked for her phone to be traced. That was when Vanguard jumped on the situation, tying it to local incidents involving militia.

The Famous Ones, whom he didn't know hardly anything about, had been nearby, and they deployed almost immediately. They'd saved her life.

So when the elevator doors opened and he was faced with

a group of women who could likely snap him in half, he smiled. "Good. I was worried she was alone."

They collectively shifted. Like a military unit that lived together, trained together, and deployed together.

One had a phone out. Petite, with jet black hair, she wasn't the kind you'd mess with. "Simon got a license plate."

The woman closest to Jasper twisted around. "We have a lead?"

The petite one nodded. "Move out." While the others grabbed bags and coats from the floor on either side of the hallway, she turned to him. "If you hurt her in any way, shape, or form, I will kill you."

He blinked. "You think no one would notice if I disappear?"

She studied him. Yes, she could definitely kill him if she wanted to. "Who says you would disappear?"

They all headed out a side door. Down the stairs? He wouldn't volunteer to walk all that way, but maybe they were making a pit stop on another floor and going down from there. Whichever it was, the whole place was a lot lighter without a crowd of deadly women milling around. They probably thought up crazy schemes when they didn't have a case to occupy them.

Jasper shut the door to the penthouse quietly, easing it closed. But Destiny wasn't on the couch. Or in the kitchen. He found a sparsely furnished office. Then, a bedroom decorated in a lot of white—not his thing, but it was classy.

The bed had been slept in, the covers shoved back. But she wasn't here.

He heard something.

"Destiny?"

She didn't reply. What if she needed someone? So, he threaded through the bedroom, then a walk-through closet, and into the well-lit room beyond. He could hear the distinct sounds of throwing up in the bathroom.

He pushed the door open.

She sat back on the floor, wiping her face with the back of her hand.

"Hey." He kept his voice soft and filled a cup at the sink. Crouching, he handed it to her. "Take slow sips."

Her face had lost some color, her lips pale. Her hand trembled, so he helped her hold the glass. There was a bandage on her cheek from where his mom had scratched her. He traced the edge of it, then stopped. This wasn't the time. "Sorry."

She lowered the cup and handed it back. "Thanks for the drink."

"Are you okay?"

What she said next was the last thing he expected.

Jasper toppled back in his crouch. His behind hit the floor, and the water cup spilled on the tile.

Tears rolled down her face.

"Pregnant?" He looked down, just a reflex. The oversized shirt. The dress that had bloused over her waist. The experience she'd had... "They raped you?"

She sobbed, burying her face in her hands.

Jasper's heart broke in his chest. He slid over and touched her head, running his hand over her hair. She lowered her hands and wrapped them around his waist, moving closer at the same time that he pulled her in and held on to her.

This took a terrible situation to a whole new level. She'd been through one of the worst things a woman could go through. Now, she would bring a life into the world. One that would remind her every day of what happened and how beauty could come from ashes.

Wasn't that the saying?

He kept his mouth shut. He'd come here to tell her... What would he even have said? How could he possibly explain? She didn't need all his family issues on top of everything else she had going on.

At least her working at Vanguard made sense. And the constant bodyguards, ready to kill for her. He understood the Famous Ones a little more now—and respected them, too.

Blake and their sisters must be...

Jasper asked, "You haven't told anyone, have you?"

Destiny pulled back, wiping her cheeks. "I need to clean up. Can we talk in the kitchen?"

He helped her to her feet and flushed the toilet for her. "Can I make you some tea? Or something to eat? I don't know what is good."

"Crackers sound good. And tea with milk? There's decaf by the kettle."

"Got it." He leaned in and kissed her forehead. "Take your time."

Jasper made sure she was steady on her feet. He walked out of that bathroom a different man than he had been when he walked in. Destiny would have a baby in a few months. In a way, that seemed like a lifetime. For her, it would probably go fast, and her life would never be the same.

Jasper stopped in the entryway to the kitchen.

Pregnant.

Destiny was going to have a baby. That realization was on repeat in his head. Walking through the door felt like moving down a path he could never retrace. Nothing would be the same.

Not for her.

Not for him.

Everything had changed.

He set the kettle to boil and raided the pantry for crackers.

He found four different kinds of cheese dip in jars and a curious amount of applesauce pouches. At least a dozen open bags of chips, and an entire section that seemed to just be flavors of fizzy water stacked in their boxes.

He made two cups of tea, and she emerged with a different set of clothes. When she came close, he smelled mint from where she'd brushed her teeth.

"Thanks for not running away screaming."

He said, "You expected the door to be open and for me to be gone?"

She shrugged. "I'm glad to see I was right about you being a better man than that." She took one of the mugs of tea over to the couch and sat, curling her legs up. "But that's because you're a good friend, a good guy. I've heard it enough from Blake. And I've seen it."

"Have you now." What should he say to that? If she knew all of it, would she still believe that? He settled on small talk and said, "Feeling better?"

"Yes." She took a drink of the tea. "Thank you for being here, even though I don't know how you got in. My sisters are calling this my fortress of solitude."

He chuckled. Maybe she was groggy and didn't remember. "I can see that. But after I texted, you had the receptionist issue me a guest pass for the elevator."

"Ah."

"What?"

She said, "I was asleep all afternoon. When you came into the bathroom, I'd only just woken up."

"So who replied to my text?"

"I can guess." She frowned. "But it was still good to see you. And thank you for your help."

Why did this sound like she was about to say goodbye?

"You're a good friend."

Yeah, he was being friend-zoned. Because he knew about the baby now? "You didn't do anything wrong. You know that, right? And this situation you're in is crazy hard, but it doesn't ruin your life. A baby will add to your family. Someone new comes into the world, and you get to love and take care of that person in a way no one else will."

Tears gathered in her eyes.

"I'm not trying to upset you. Sorry. I'm just letting you know there is always good and bad in everything."

"You don't have to stay." She brushed at the loose sweats over her knees. "I'm good. Thanks."

"I know I don't have to." He wasn't going *anywhere*. "Destiny? Do you want me to stay?"

The look in her eyes told him she knew he didn't mean only now.

He just might mean forever.

He'd have to tell her everything, but after what she just shared and the courage she showed every day, she had the ability to weather what was in front of her. The fact was, for a while now, he'd known something poignant.

It was her.

She was the one.

What might look to anyone from the outside like a rebound, after the mess he'd left Tessa in, the reality was that he'd been searching for the right thing for a long time.

He was about to prompt her when she said, "Yes. If you want to, I want you to stay."

Jasper leaned over so their faces were close. "I want to stay."

He couldn't let her be unsure. Not with everything she was about to face. She had to know he would be there for her.

No matter what.

FOURTEEN

Destiny's stomach had settled enough between the tea and crackers. What she really wanted was popcorn. She put a package in the microwave, even though everyone said it was terrible for you. She needed comfort right now.

And a minute out of Jasper's immediate vicinity to breathe.

She sent a text to the Famous Ones chat.

You let him up? Really?

All she got back were emojis, so apparently, they thought that was an adequate answer. It was easier to be irritated than to face her situation—and the man who'd settled himself on her couch. He probably wanted to talk through it all, but she might not have the energy. When the popcorn was done, she poured it in a bowl and took it back over, placing it between them.

She sat facing him, her legs crossed on the seat. Mr. Fancy Suit Police Detective kicked off his shoes and put his suit jacket on the recliner chair. He even loosened his tie and pulled it over his head. "You don't have to get back to work?"

"Not today. I've clocked enough hours, and with the witness downstairs in protective custody, I can be on hand in case anything happens."

"You don't want to go back to your house and get some actual rest instead of hanging out with a cranky, nauseous pregnant woman."

"I'm not touching that one." He tossed a handful of popcorn into his mouth.

Destiny had to ask. "Is your mom all right?"

"That's a simple question that should have a simple answer, but instead, it's..." Jasper fell silent for a minute, and she got to study him in profile. Did he even know he was basically breathtaking?

Probably, he'd realized by now that women fell over themselves to get to him. Her sisters had talked about him at length. And the waitresses at Backdraft where she used to work before...

She didn't want to think about that.

"My mom," he began. "When she found out Tessa and I were engaged, she told me that if I didn't break it off, she would kill herself."

Destiny stilled her hand over the popcorn bowl.

"She had problems with me dating. It was why I waited weeks to tell her I was even engaged. She doesn't attend many public events, and we managed to keep it from her." The skin around his eyes flexed. "We manage a lot with her. And for her. So this wasn't any different. She was civil enough to Tessa the couple of times they met. But something Tessa's father—he's the deputy mayor—had said to my mom around a decade ago made her dig her heels in."

He took a deep breath. "And when I say that, I mean I

came over to check on mom, and she was in the bathtub. She'd slit her wrists and nearly drowned while she was bleeding to death."

Destiny laid her hand on his knee. "I'm so sorry."

"Because you have compassion. Something my mom has never had." He tipped his head to the side. "Well, maybe she had it before…"

"Before Caleb?"

He hesitated. "My father told you about him?"

Destiny squeezed his knee. "You had a brother?"

"He was my best friend." Jasper squeezed the bridge of his nose. "And then, he was just…gone, and everything was so empty. Maybe she wasn't like this before he got sick, but I don't remember her ever being other than what she is now."

"I'm sorry she believes I tried to kill her."

Jasper looked at her, a curious expression on his face. "You really mean that."

"Of course. She deserves our compassion."

"Sometimes, I don't have much left to draw from." He blew out a breath. "It's been running low, and I can see my dad is starting to feel the same way. He hasn't outright said we should admit her where she can live in a beautiful place but also be taken care of around the clock. But I also realize that makes me sound like a horrible person."

"In the end, it's up to your father to make the final decision."

Jasper's expression started to crack. "He said it wasn't my choice to be part of this family. It was his. So what happened next would be his choice, too."

"I really like your dad."

He cleared his throat. "Thanks."

She decided to just go for the gusto. "Jamal was my father. That's how your father and I got to talking about Caleb. And probably why neither of us realized there was a sniper in the trees." She slid down the couch and put her head back on the cushion, suddenly cold. "I thought I was going to die."

She'd thought Jasper's mother was dead.

Richard could have died.

Her baby.

Destiny swiped at her cheek. "Stupid hormones."

"I'm glad you weren't hurt. Apart from." He motioned to her cheek.

"She's sick. It makes a lot more sense now."

He slid down the couch as well, resting the back of his head against the back cushion so that he'd be facing the TV— if it were on. She was comfortable enough that it was like they'd done this a million times.

When in reality, they'd never been alone in either of their houses. They'd never been on a date. They were from two different worlds, but that seemed to matter less and less. And now, here, where they were alone, it was like it didn't matter at all.

"I shouldn't want to hide away and never go out. I should be stronger than that."

He glanced over. "I think you're doing great."

"Blake said I should want people around me."

Humor gleamed in his eyes. "I'm people."

She gave him a soft smile.

"The Famous Ones are on the case, looking for whoever shot at you. Or shot at my parents. I guess when they find the shooter, we'll know who the target was." He paused. "I think for the time being, maybe you *should* stay where it's safe. Just in case."

"Are you going to tell your parents to do the same?"

He smiled. "I will if it makes you feel better."

Being here was so nice and comfortable, Destiny could

almost forget the tiny bump in her abdomen was a baby. She was still "pretty small," according to Clare, but the naturally round belly she'd always had played into it. No one had guessed. She'd kept everyone at arm's length since she got back, but that wouldn't last forever.

"Everyone is going to flip. They'll want to know why I didn't say anything."

Jasper reached over and took her hand, resting it on the couch by the popcorn bowl. "I can be with you when you tell them."

Destiny groaned. "Everything is just all mixed up. It should be getting better or back to normal or something. But it's never going to be normal again. I'm going to have a child. Jasper, I'm *terrified*. I don't know how to be a mom! What if I'm awful at it? My mom was the worst."

He squeezed her hand. "The fact you care enough to worry already has you a step ahead. I'm not worried. I know it won't be easy for you, but I don't doubt you'll be a great mom."

She suppressed another groan. He was being so sweet that she was going to get used to it, and then he was going to leave. They would be friends. She would get bigger, give birth. Jasper would find someone. He would fall in love, and she'd have to watch him have a family with someone else.

Someone better than her.

Right now, he was all in to be supportive, and that was amazing. But she couldn't tie up his life with her stuff. He had work responsibilities. The last thing he would want to do is take on a baby that was the result of pain and terror like she'd never experienced—and wouldn't wish on her worst enemy.

Over on the breakfast bar, her phone buzzed to life, vibrating and ringing on the countertop.

"I'll grab it." Jasper hopped up and fetched it for her.

Don't get used to it. That would only make it twice as hard when he took all that goodness and pulled away from her. The right thing, but it would be a loss.

"This says *System Breach*," he said. "What does that mean?"

She held out her hand, and he put the phone in it. "Nothing good." She dialed Simon's number and put the call on speaker.

"I know, I know," Simon answered. "I see it."

"What's going on?"

"Someone hacked the Vanguard network, and they're rooting through our system."

"How is that possible?" Destiny asked. "I thought we were air-gapped and secure and all that tech stuff."

"There's only one explanation." Simon paused long enough she nearly prompted him. "They're inside the building."

She glanced at Jasper, who said, "Not me." As if she'd been thinking that.

Destiny said, "I'll call Clare."

FIFTEEN

"I go first. Remember?" Jasper touched her shoulder before she could go through the doorway. They'd come down a different elevator, much smaller than the regular one.

"It's just Clare's office." She stepped aside, though.

"The person with the gun goes first." Protecting the person who is pregnant.

He still could hardly believe it. He'd told her about Caleb, and for the first time in years, he could share his memories of his brother with someone. The whole deal with his mom? Different mountain to climb.

"This is about me being pregnant, isn't it?"

"Honestly? Yeah." He opened the door to Clare's office and saw the lights had been dimmed and the door was shut. No one lurked around. But then, this attack was over the network. Not a physical breach. There were no bad guys to fight here.

Even so, he wasn't going to take any chances with her safety.

And the fact she could discuss it like this showed how far

she'd come in the past couple of months. He had a million questions but didn't know much about pregnancy. Jasper realized Gage probably knew.

Blake was going to hit the roof when he found out two of his friends had known. Men he considered brothers—family. Exactly the family Jasper had needed to find within SWAT. Blake would consider withholding the truth a betrayal.

"I'll stay here and..." She trailed off.

"Do Vanguard things?" Ones she had to sign a nondisclosure agreement for? Maybe Gage had signed one that kept him from telling Blake about the baby. Could they get one retroactively dated so Jasper could argue he hadn't been able to tell his friend that his sister was pregnant?

"Are you okay?"

She must've picked up on his frustration or worry. He said, "I need to go find Simon. You're staying here?"

She was already at Clare's desk, switching on the computer. Her phone on the surface of the desk flashed. Beeps sounded in rapid succession. "I can lock the doors after you leave. And there's a panic room. I'm good."

"I'll leave you to it." He waited until he'd turned away before he grinned. He guessed she might not think she had the qualifications to be in the job she'd landed, but she looked natural behind the desk. Almost like she belonged there.

She'd come a long way in the weeks since arriving home. Since he'd shown up at the hospital, and she screamed at him to get out.

Now he knew what that had been about.

His chest squeezed, and he rubbed at his breastbone where the grief he felt for Caleb lived. Where he carried memories of his brother in his heart. Tucked away. Caleb would've been Destiny's biggest fan.

Jasper threaded through the office and spotted Simon, and

his brother, Peter, standing beside his chair. Both of them stared intently at Simon's computer screen.

Jasper asked, "Someone breached your network?"

Peter straightened. "He's narrowing it down." The twin who was an operative walked to a metal cabinet against the wall and flipped the door latch. "You have your gun?"

Jasper patted his hip.

Peter handed him a radio with the earpiece connected by a wire. "Channel three. Whoever hacked us is in the building, and we're gonna go find them." He looked almost gleeful, but this was the part of the job he'd decided to settle on.

Peter had a woman in his life, and Jasper had heard they were setting a date to get married in the summer.

Blake, Liam, Gage. Even River, though Jasper probably wouldn't go to that wedding since he was allergic to dogs. His friends had all found someone, they'd fallen in love. One by one, he'd seen them go head over heels.

He'd thought it wouldn't happen for him because Destiny left. Then, she'd been back and wanted nothing to do with him.

Now, there was a baby to consider.

A lot of conversations about what she had planned, what she wanted. What he wanted. It wasn't the type of situation they could simply jump into, even if part of him didn't mind doing that at all. Why not help her? But if he didn't tread carefully, she'd believe his attention was about sympathy for her predicament. She wouldn't know it was because he'd been half in love with her for months.

Every new thing he learned about her convinced him she was amazing. Finding out she was pregnant changed nothing.

Simon said, "The training center."

"Come on." Peter led him to the stairway, and they hustled it up the stairs. "Destiny okay?"

"She's in Clare's office." And he wouldn't have left her if she wasn't all right. Peter had a woman in his life, so he knew. "How many people are in this building?"

"The Cold Case team was in a meeting, that's how I happened to be here. But there aren't many others. Reception. Maybe one or two more."

"And the apartments upstairs?"

"Three are occupied. The guy in seven isn't going anywhere. Your confidential informant and Destiny are the only ones staying overnight aside from the security guard."

Better not to ask about the guy in seven, or he'd end up having to sign one of those NDAs. "Is the building security guard up here?"

Peter shook his head. "He stays downstairs on the surveillance cameras. His job is the doors."

Whatever that meant. "All right. Then let's find this hacker."

Peter went first into what was a gym. Weight machines and cardio machines along one wall. A fighting ring, and a huge expansive area with two inches of mat on the floor. "Don't walk on that with your shoes unless you have to."

"Got it." Jasper didn't see anyone in the room besides them.

"Go right. I'll go left and check the locker rooms. You get storage."

They split up. Peter disappeared into a room on the left side. Jasper swept over to the corner and a door marked Storage. Instead of cleaning supplies and towels, he found gear that could be used to storm a building. He even spotted some nunchucks, whatever that was about.

Maybe they would be useful later. Clare had asked him to train Destiny. Since he planned to spend a whole lot of time with her for the foreseeable future, they could work on some things. He could teach her how to protect herself.

Knowing now what she'd been through, he should have suggested it before. Every woman should know how to defend herself—same with every man. No one wanted to be vulnerable. That didn't mean turning into the aggressor in a situation. It just meant you had skills that could save your life.

He spotted a door at the back of the closet and opened that. Inside were mop buckets and cleaning supplies.

His radio crackled to life, and Peter said, "Nothing in the locker rooms. Jasper?"

"Storage is clear."

"Sie?"

The twin's voice came through, sounding exactly like Peter's so that it was going to be impossible to tell them apart. "They moved. This is..." He let out a sound of frustration. "Above you."

"The staging area?" Peter asked.

"No," Simon said, "there's a terminal on the west side. Halfway down, in the wall."

Jasper jogged around the training mat back to the stairs. Peter met him there. Jasper went first, upstairs. "This floor?"

Peter said, "Hook left."

This hallway appeared to be a whole lot more industrial. At the bend, he looked first before stepping out. The woman had a laptop plugged into an open panel on the wall, her attention on the screen.

Jasper held his gun up and took measured steps down the hall. "April, put the computer on the floor, and put your hands up."

She let out a sharp noise and nearly dropped the laptop.

"Put it down."

Peter followed right behind him. "You're done here."

April sneered. "Yeah, I am." She dropped the laptop horizontally so that it hit the linoleum flat. Shattered from the sound of it. Had she just destroyed evidence? She raised her hands. "Guess you caught me."

Something about this raised the hair on Jasper's arms. "You're coming with us."

The woman had injuries from being "beaten" by her boyfriend. But had the plan all along been to infiltrate Vanguard and access it from the inside?

Jasper got her cuffed and then pulled out his phone while she faced the wall with her hands secured behind her back. He dialed Samantha's number.

"Detective Jesse."

"Your confidential informant is under arrest," Jasper explained.

"I'm on my way." Samantha hung up.

He stowed his phone and glanced at Peter, who was also on the phone. The guy had a dark look on his face. "What's the damage to Vanguard? What did she access?"

They could have assets that were now compromised.

"He doesn't know." Peter stowed his phone. "Yet."

April started to laugh.

SIXTEEN

Destiny clicked her mouse in the program window on their secure network. "Okay, I got it."

Through the phone speaker on the desk, Clare said, "Type this." She rattled off a long series of letters, numbers, and symbols. "Then hit enter."

"Done."

The computer screen flashed COMPLETE.

"That should secure everything."

More like quadruple secure, but she got the point. Destiny said, "Jasper knows."

"You told him?"

She lifted the handset and sat back in the chair, holding the phone to her ear. "The Famous Ones let him up, and he found me in the bathroom doing my regular post nap puking."

"How is your stomach?"

"I'm all right." But she would need some soup or something soon. Did Jasper want to get dinner? He probably wanted "real" food, not one of the few things her stomach could keep down. But she loved ordering from that place around the corner that did sandwiches, salads, and soups.

As long as Vanguard remained secure, she would be all right.

At least, that was what it felt like to her. Probably since she lived here, their team had saved her, and they'd given her a place to be safe—for as long as she wanted.

Destiny bit her lip. "I need to tell Blake and my sisters."

Clare didn't answer right away. "They caught her."

Her?

Before Destiny could ask who the hacker was, Clare said, "Invite them all over for dinner. Get lots of dessert, and after you tell them, when everyone is crying, bring out the cake."

Destiny started to chuckle.

"It's going to be hard. But they love you, and they will support you. Do you think the girls won't go crazy over a baby niece or nephew? You'll have so much help you won't know what to do with it."

She smiled—something that didn't happen for weeks after she got back. These days, her joy was coming more often. Especially when she was around Jasper. "He didn't run screaming."

"Because he's a good man."

"I'm not going to trap him into feeling like he needs to help me emotionally or help me take care of this baby. That's not why I told him." Destiny hadn't had much choice. He'd have told everyone she was sick, but it was better this way. He knew why she'd screamed at him. Why she worked at Vanguard. Why they could be friends.

But nothing more.

A guy like Jasper deserved an easy relationship that didn't add more baggage. Not someone who'd been abused and would always have with her the result of her nightmare. She could hold herself together without falling apart. If he stuck around her, they would both have to confront what happened.

Bad enough with her family, but they loved her, and she could deal with their pity. Jasper...

If only he could see her as strong and capable. The kind of woman he deserved.

Instead, her feet were going to swell. She was going to be dealing with a newborn, not wearing a dress like she had the other night or attending fabulous events. She would be a mom.

"Why don't you let him decide?" Clare asked.

"He's a good guy," Destiny argued. "He'll stick around because he feels sorry for me, and he knows I need help. And I'll know that's why he's still here." Even so, it might be too much for her to nurse heartbreak at what she couldn't have at the same time she nursed a baby.

"God put him in your life for a reason."

What if that reason was to show her what she couldn't have? What she shouldn't wish for? Maybe that wasn't fair, but God hadn't answered her prayers on this. Yet.

The door to the office opened, and Simon stuck his head in. "Conference room." He hesitated. "You good?"

Destiny hung up with Clare and stood. "I'm good. I just need to talk to Blake." She got on the family text thread and sent a message.

> Family meeting. Sunday dinner, in the
> Vanguard penthouse.

She stowed her phone. She could check for replies and reactions later, after they talked with the hacker.

In the conference room, Peter and Jasper stood on either side of the woman that he and his partner had brought into Vanguard.

"April, isn't it?"

The woman shot her a sardonic look. Early twenties,

bruised up with a split lip. Her eyes were fire. "That part was true."

Detective Jesse showed up.

Simon stepped out of the room to admit her. "Sam."

"Sie."

They grinned at each other. Friends? That was interesting. Peter lifted his chin.

Samantha faced the seated woman. "I thought we said no lies."

April snorted. "Worked, didn't it? You gave me cash. You got me in here when I needed it."

"And now you need to not go to jail," Samantha said. "Trust me, you won't like it."

"Don't care." The woman sniffed.

"Why access the Vanguard network?"

Simon shifted his weight, probably wanting an answer to the question.

"My business." April leaned to the side so she could ask Simon, "Don't you know what I did in your system?"

He said nothing.

"How about you tell us what you did?" Jasper asked.

Destiny waved Simon out into the hall. She kept her voice low and asked, "Do we know what she accessed?" If there was an issue with the network, he'd be fixing it, not hanging around to see what April said.

He shook his head. "I mean, not technically. She accessed the entire system. Walked in like it was nothing."

"Did she copy any files? Would you be able to tell that?"

"I have the laptop she was using. I only got a quick chance to look, but she seems to have launched a program that erased everything on the device when she was caught."

"So she accounted for the possibility of being caught." Destiny didn't like the sound of that. "She got herself beaten up on purpose to make it look like she needed protection so she could be brought here."

And at nearly the same time, someone had shot at the senator. Or her. Or perhaps the target had been Jasper's mother.

She needed to touch base with the Famous Ones and find out how the hunt for the shooter was going.

Destiny blew out a breath. "Okay, go see if you can find out what she did. If she didn't take anything, maybe she left something."

Simon flinched. He spun around, muttering as he ran for his desk.

The last thing they needed was a virus. Or a backdoor for someone else to come in and mess with the system—potentially without anyone knowing.

Back at the door to the conference room, she watched as Samantha reached for April's arm. "Come on. Let's go. You're going to jail."

Peter said, "Hold up. She's not going anywhere until we know what she did."

"He's right," Destiny said. "We may need her here to undo whatever she caused."

April grinned. "Who knows *what* damage I did to their precious system."

Destiny wasn't sure about this girl whose demeanor didn't ring true. Behind the smugness was something else, and she couldn't put her finger on what it was.

Jasper glanced between April and Destiny. "She's being arrested. You guys can't hang on to her indefinitely. She has the right to a lawyer."

Peter saved her from having to answer. "What if we don't want to press charges? Maybe this was nothing but an innocent mistake."

April eyed Peter. "I don't make mistakes."

"Quiet." Samantha glanced over her shoulder at Destiny. "I get that you might need her to fix something or tell you what she did, but that might not happen without due process. And I doubt you want her messing with your system more than she already has."

"That's not up to me." Destiny looked at the screen of her phone. "Clare is on her way up. She'll decide what is going to happen with this woman."

Jasper said, "She's being arrested."

"She's my CI." Samantha wasn't going to back down any more than Jasper looked prepared to. "I brought her here. I'll deal with her."

"This wasn't your fault," Jasper said. "You couldn't have known she would do this."

So much compassion. Seeing it in him now reminded her of exactly why she had to steel herself against his goodness and be strong. Take care of things on her own. If she gave him an inch, he would be all in for miles of helping her with the baby. And how could she, in all good conscience, do that to a guy who needed to be free to fall in love. Get married.

Samantha said, "It *is* my fault."

April snorted.

"Guess I know now what kind of woman you are." Samantha folded her arms. "And I was epically wrong about you."

Simon appeared at the door. "I know what she did." He looked at April. "Draconem."

Peter flinched.

April shrugged, but for a second, Destiny saw fear in her eyes. "Guess you caught me."

So why did it seem like she wanted to be in cuffs?

"That's a good idea." In truth, Jasper had been thinking the same thing. But now that Peter had suggested they go talk to April's boyfriend—the one who had supposedly beaten her up and the reason she'd needed protection—Jasper couldn't say he'd had the same idea, or it would only look like he was trying to one-up the Vanguard operative.

Given the tenuous situation right now, he couldn't posture. Even if it was true.

Simon had found a file buried in their system. Password protected, possibly some kind of virus waiting to be set off like a bomb.

Jasper hopped off the edge of the desk, far too aware of Destiny across the bullpen talking to Clare. "Peter and I are going to go talk to April's boyfriend."

Samantha still had her CI in the conference room. Trying to convince her to talk about what she'd been doing here. Not arresting her—yet—meant they didn't have to offer her counsel. However, she could choose to not say anything at all. Which seemed to be April's tactic so far.

Just a whole lot of attitude and no confession.

Clare tugged out a chair so she could sit. "Thank you. Destiny and I have a few fires to put out."

Simon didn't look up from his computer. Gage had dropped off Clare but hadn't stayed. The team from Cold Cases had been in and out, offering help. One or two of them could come up and back up Samantha, given the alternative was a computer guy with a lot of work ahead of him and two pregnant women.

He suggested the idea to Peter, not wanting the women to think they were taking care of them. Even if that's exactly what it was.

"Good idea." He picked up a desk phone and dialed three numbers. "Couple people for backup in the bullpen. Jasper and I are going out." Peter listened for a second, then hung up. "They're coming."

"Good. Let's go." He told Samantha what they were doing and confirmed the guy's information and a couple of places they might find him, then leaned down and kissed Destiny's cheek. "If I don't end up coming back, I'll call you later."

Generally, he never knew how a day was going to go. He couldn't make a guarantee he'd be back, but it wasn't like he would leave here and forget the magnitude of what she'd told him. Neither would he stop caring about her.

She squeezed his elbow. Nearly said something.

He'd ask her about that later. Maybe without an audience.

Jasper drove to the bar where Samantha had seemed sure they would find the boyfriend at this time on a Saturday.

Peter made a "huh" sound with his head bent over his tablet. The guy was as astute at computer stuff as his brother, he just chose to be out of the office more than in it. Jasper could respect that. There were parts of his job he liked better than others.

But coming home to Destiny at the end of the day?

That just might end up being the best part.

He wasn't completely convinced, all in, determined to be a father to this baby and the only man she was with for the rest of her life. There were a lot of things to talk about. He needed to address the issue of his parents, though his father would probably be nothing but supportive.

His mother, on the other hand.

He'd have to work on a solution so his mother didn't get hurt because of his choices. She wouldn't have a relationship with her grandchildren—if or when he had any kids. But he didn't want her to harm herself.

Peter said, "This guy Franks is a peach."

"Yeah?" Jasper turned onto the street where the bar was located. Rough part of town. Rough guy. Rough bar, sandwiched between a vape shop and a couple of closed-down businesses. The parking lot was full of trucks and motorcycles.

He parked the car at the far end of the lot.

"Neal did four years for aggravated assault, got released early. Behind on his child support. He's thirty-two and has fifteen- and sixteen-year-old sons. Two other younger kids with another woman." Peter glanced over. "Isn't April like twenty-two?"

Jasper shrugged. Destiny was a few years younger than him. "I try not to be judgy."

"According to this, he lives above his grandmother's garage and works at a mechanic shop. The reviews on the shop are worse than the reviews on the bar. Apparently, they like to charge people and not do the work."

Jasper shut off the engine. "Great. Let's go see what he has to say about April."

The place had a couple of handfuls of people. At the bar

and over by the pool tables. There was a game on above the bar in the corner, baseball being played by an East Coast team. No one really seemed to be paying attention to it.

They seemed more attuned to the badge on Jasper's belt.

Before they could all make a run for it, he said, "Neal Franks."

A few people relaxed. Someone said, "Back there by the games."

Slot machines, a couple of arcade machines. All of which were not completely legal. He spotted a machine that would dispense scratch-off tickets. Neal Franks was playing a retro game and losing, by the look of it.

The whole bar smelled like puke on a carpet mixed with stale beer.

When he let out a frustrated curse word and stepped back, Jasper said, "Neal Franks?"

He flinched and turned to them. There was a split second when he seemed to consider making a run for it. But with Peter to the left, there was nowhere for him to go without him having to fight one of them. Which would end up with him back in the system.

"This isn't about you," Jasper said. "It's about April."

He made a face and grabbed the half-empty beer glass from the table. "Her?" He downed the remainder of his drink. "What about her?"

Peter asked, "When was the last time you saw her?"

Neal shrugged. "Weeks ago."

Interesting, considering she'd told him and Samantha that it was Neal who'd beat her. "She ever talk about Vanguard?"

Neal shook his head. "That company with the tower?" He glanced at Peter. "You're one of them?"

He almost looked scared by the possibility that Peter was with Vanguard.

Interesting.

"Do you have reason to be worried about Vanguard?" Jasper asked. "Like being a part of a scheme to break into their computer network."

Neal cracked a laugh. "Do I look stupid? Not nearly worth the trouble."

"Have you heard anyone talk about something like that?"

"No way." Neal waved a hand.

"What about April?"

"Who knows what she is up to? I said I haven't seen her." He kicked out a chair and slumped into it.

"Any idea of where she went after you parted ways?" Jasper asked.

"Her dad came back to town. She was pretty spun up about that, wanting to drop everything and go see him. I don't play that way."

"Families?" Not a surprise, what with the backlog of child support payments.

"She got all wound up about him, cleaning up to impress him. Probably lookin' for a payout. She needed the money since she screwed up the last job she took."

Peter asked, "What does she do?"

"Computer...something."

That made sense with the hacking skills. But who would go up against Vanguard—and Simon? All to leave something in their network.

Neal shrugged. "She was always on her laptop."

"Who did she work for?"

"Some guy." Another shrug.

"Any idea who it was?" Jasper had to tamp down his frustration. When Neal shook his head, Jasper said, "Pay your child support."

They walked out the front door and back to the car. On

the way, his phone started to ring. But it wasn't an incoming call, it was an alert on the PD system. "There's an incident going down. They need armed response."

"Let's go."

Maybe not such a good plan to show up with Peter, but at least the guy knew how to handle himself—and stay out of the way of police business. SWAT needed to respond as soon as they could assemble.

He read off the address. "That's George Anderson's house."

Something was happening with Violet's father.

Peter got back on his laptop while Jasper drove with lights and sirens on. The Vanguard operative said, "Reports of shots fired. Neighbor called it in, multiple assailants."

EIGHTEEN

"All I can say is thank goodness I had a nap."

Clare glanced over, grinning. She squeezed Destiny's shoulder. "The fatigue gets better. In the middle, when you get less sick, you'll find you have more energy."

She touched her front, right over her belt—currently a hole looser than she'd worn it before she left for Africa. "Any updates on Jasper's mother?"

"Still thinking about her?"

She glanced at the wall of windows between the break room and the bullpen. Two guys from Cold Cases had come up, and apparently, Samantha or Jasper called the PD because a couple of uniformed officers had arrived. One of them was Romeo Alvarez, Simon's friend. Officer Alvarez had eaten at Backdraft a lot when she worked there, and Simon had joined him.

Little had she known, just before Christmas, that she would be working as Clare's executive assistant now. Having a baby, like her boss.

It still seemed so bizarre that her life had turned into this.

Clare said, "I'll ask Richard how she's doing." She typed on her phone.

Destiny drank some of her tea, which Clare had made for both of them. When Clare was done, Destiny tried to figure out how to ask her question.

"What is it?"

Of course, her boss had picked up on it. "I really felt like God told me to go to Africa."

"Because He did." Clare seemed so sure. "You heard Him."

Destiny held on to her mug, warming her hands. "Why would He send me if He knew what was going to happen?"

"You might never know."

"What if that's not a good enough answer?" God had allowed what happened to her to occur, but He hadn't orchestrated it. People had free will. The man who attacked her had done so because he *could*, and if anyone was behind it, then it was the enemy of every believer. Not God.

"Why do people die of cancer? Why are children sold?" Clare asked.

"Because we live in a fallen world."

"Do we have to understand the why of the pain to find the depth of comfort in healing?" Clare gave her a long look. "You may never have peace with what happened to you, but you can trust God to bring you through all of this. And to give you wisdom for the future."

Jasper.

That's what Clare was talking about. "He doesn't need to be saddled with me and a baby he never asked for."

Clare made a face. "What if that's exactly what he needs?"

"No way." Destiny shook her head. "It's not even what I need, but it happened."

Clare's expression said she wasn't sure that was true. Her phone buzzed, and she lifted the device to see the screen since leaning forward wasn't an option right now.

Something Destiny wasn't exactly anticipating. Though, getting sick every day was worse.

"SWAT was deployed to George Anderson's house. Reports of shots fired." Clare shifted in her seat.

She clearly wanted to go but shouldn't. Better for the pregnant woman to stay out of the way than risk being hurt. Despite her nature, Clare was channeling that need to wade into the fray toward caring for the child growing in her.

Destiny had never desired to be a cop, or an operative. But she felt the same need to protect the life growing inside her, even if it was barely the size of a plum.

Clare said, "Unlock your phone and open the app. I'll give you a crash course in operations while we distract ourselves because our men are in danger."

"This says Brent Rammington wants to meet."

"Right." Clare tapped the screen on her phone, and the notification on Destiny's was marked accepted. "So we send him some options on times, and he accepts the slot he wants. We've got two requests from Europe, which you'll pass to Mack. Badger's wife thinks she saw a high-value target when they were on vacation last week. We can have Peter look into it, and if there's something there, then he can follow up."

The amount of things Clare coordinated blew Destiny's mind on a regular basis, but the reality was that she employed the best and she delegated amazingly—all from her phone.

If she wanted to take on a mission, she could. If she wanted to stay home with the baby, she could.

"Why do I feel like you're gearing up to have me cover for you when you have the baby?"

Clare grinned. "I'm sure everyone in the company will pitch in if you need it."

"I'll be terrified. You have no idea."

"Oh, I think I have an idea." Clare tipped her head to the side. "Except the idea of Jasper wanting to spend more time with you is scarier than this." She motioned to the phone. "Right?"

"So, the notifications."

Clare laughed.

Destiny enjoyed another chance to smile, even in the middle of everything. She took a moment and closed her eyes, praying silently for the SWAT team. For Violet's father, George. That the whole situation would be resolved without bloodshed. God's will would be done, and that didn't always mean success. Or that there would be no pain.

She knew that better than anyone.

He may have allowed her to be attacked, but that wouldn't be what He'd *wanted* to happen. His perfect will would see peace on earth—the kind that would only come in heaven. She asked for that perfect will in this situation, knowing that the faith of a child of God was enough to change hearts. Because unless people submitted to Him, there was only so much He could do—that gray area between God being able to act and giving humans the free will to choose how much power they allowed God to have over them.

She still hadn't fully worked it out.

Maybe no one ever did. Too many people skewed it the wrong way, to their own ends. Wanting to be the lord over their own lives. They didn't even acknowledge God, let alone allow Him to lead and direct them.

If He had brought her here, then it was for His purposes. There was something that He would use her situation for. So that she could be a witness for His goodness.

If Jasper was meant to be a part of this, then there was a reason for that, too. She didn't want him to feel trapped. Though, if she was honest with herself, she did feel trapped, in a way, by what had happened to her. And the baby that resulted. It wasn't the way a child was supposed to come into the world.

But if God could be seen through her, then her whole goal of going to Africa had been fulfilled. Not exactly the answer to her prayer that she'd expected. But God's will would continue to be seen as long as this child was alive.

Both of their phones buzzed.

"Simon." He needed them to come to his station.

"Peter sent him intel."

Destiny pushed her chair back, and the two pregnant ladies went to the bullpen. She couldn't even see April because there were so many people by the door. Cops. Vanguard agents. The blinds had been closed, so Samantha wasn't visible, either.

Simon turned in his chair. "Based on what Peter and Jasper found out from the ex-boyfriend who supposedly beat up April, we looked at her relatives and discovered that the only one living is her father. They're estranged, by all appearances, and he has no trace of employment. Decades ago, he paid cash for the house she lives in and secured a trust fund for her that pays out monthly. Though, it's due to run out in three years if he doesn't add to the balance."

Clare asked, "Who is he?"

"No record of him in any database. No driver's license. No indication he was ever employed by the government or started a business on his own."

Destiny frowned. "How do we even know he exists?"

Both of them looked at her. Clare grinned. "That's a good question."

Okay, then. Maybe she was getting the hang of this.

Simon said, "A couple of photos on her social media accounts. None of them had his entire face, but I pieced it together like assembling a fingerprint from several partials. I ran that through the FBI database and got a hit."

"Who is he?" Clare asked, flipping her phone over and over on her leg. Probably waiting for word from Gage on how the SWAT callout went.

She was *not* going to do the same while waiting to hear from Jasper.

Simon said, "He's got a watch on him, but no one has a name. Only an image drawn by a forensic artist based on a witness sketch of the man who murdered her husband. No one knows who he is, but every lettered agency wants him found."

Clare's hand stilled, a white-knuckle grip on the cell. "So, what did April leave on the Vanguard system?"

"A file I still can't access. But I think she put it there for safekeeping."

NINETEEN

"Something isn't right." Jasper stomped the heel of his boot on the floor to dislodge whatever was under his sock. He held his weapon to his chest with the strap across his body and the barrel pointed down. He stood in the entryway of George Anderson's house.

The gunfight had been a few warning shots. Thankfully, SWAT had responded in time to prevent any loss of life.

George was good for now, but he couldn't stay here.

After what had happened with April, the hacker, he couldn't suggest a safe house apartment at Vanguard. If something went wrong, it would be on him again. But this was Violet's father.

His SWAT buddy Blake sat with George—who would be his father-in-law soon enough—talking quietly over what had happened. Two other SWAT officers and several patrol cops had four gangbangers against the wall in the hallway, cuffed and waiting for transport.

"What'd you say?" Gage stowed his phone.

"Something isn't right." Jasper turned, trying to figure out if what niggled at him was in his peripheral. "This whole situation."

What was making him feel like this was off? Maybe the whole thing. Someone showing up at George's house, making a whole lot of noise. Drawing far too much attention to him. If the kingpin wanted him dead, it would've been a lot easier to do it quietly.

Maybe it had something to do with his parents and Destiny and which one had been targeted at the cemetery. The shooter got away, and he was still out there.

Gage asked, "You think it's a misdirection?"

His lieutenant didn't want an answer if Jasper didn't have one, so he just shrugged.

If this was some kind of diversion, there was no telling what this guy might be up to. The kingpin seemed to have so many things going on, making it that much harder to nail him down. Scooping up territory was one thing. Messing with a business leader and a senator? Something different.

Then, there were the gunmen themselves—the ones SWAT now had in cuffs. The possibility that these men had participated in that massacre of cops a couple of months ago was something they'd have to unpack after the fact. No one wanted cop killers to get away with it.

Vanguard thought handing the police information about a financial transaction would've solved it. But maybe not.

"Where are we at on the incident at Rammington-Harper?" Jasper asked.

"FBI took the case so their forensic accountants can figure out where the money went."

"We need to ID this kingpin." Jasper couldn't let go of the anxiety. "And we need to watch ourselves on the way out of here."

Anderson called out, "I'm not staying here. I need protection."

Gage ignored the man and said to Jasper, "Your tension could just be residual, left over from the church."

Jasper bristled at the insinuation he was having a trauma reaction from the massacre outside the church a couple of months ago. Not that there was anything wrong with having a trauma reaction. He just didn't like the idea of it affecting his behavior.

A half dozen people had died, most of them cops. Gage's suggestion was completely reasonable. "It might be that. I just don't think it is." *And I don't want it to be.*

Gage nodded. "Okay. We'll watch ourselves."

Jasper shifted his weight, trying to get rid of the adrenaline racing through his system.

"How was everything over at Vanguard?" Gage glanced at Blake, then back at Jasper.

He knows about Destiny. He had to, considering Clare was his wife. Jasper said, "They're good." He needed to let out at least a little of what he was feeling. "Blake is gonna hit the roof when he finds out everything that happened to her."

"But she chose to include you in it."

Might not be so cut and dry as that. "Those women, the Famous Ones, let me up. She had no idea I'd be coming over. But I'm glad she told me. I wanna be there to help."

"You get what that means, right?" Gage's expression darkened. "Don't string her along and break her heart, thinking you're helping out, but you're hurting her more, and you don't even realize."

Jasper clenched his back teeth. "You think I—"

"What's going on?" Blake stood beside them.

Jasper said, "Nothing." To Gage, he said, "I've got it covered."

"Yeah?" Gage said. "Like you did with Tessa?"

So he would try to help and end up making things worse? The guys didn't know the truth about how it had gone down with Tessa. They didn't know about Caleb.

In fact, maybe they didn't know him all that well. Because he hadn't let them in.

No surprise now that he had to deal with the fact they'd come to their own conclusions.

"You don't know anything about me and Tessa," Jasper pointed out.

"So tell us," Blake said. "You've never explained it."

"Because I didn't think I needed to justify myself to the people I work with."

Blake flinched. Jasper knew that sounded rude, and he didn't like it any more than Blake did.

Gage said, "That's all we are to you?"

No, but it wasn't the point. "You know what I mean. We're brothers. But that's my life, and you wouldn't understand." And he had zero desire to get into it right now.

"You realize how long we've been waiting for you to actually explain it?" Blake asked.

"This isn't the time." Jasper headed for the front door and looked out. "Transport is here."

The officers on hand escorted the shooters outside. Four gangbangers who had come here to throw their weight around, terrify George Anderson, and what? Scare him into not telling the police what he knew?

George was one of the few people in Benson who knew what the kingpin looked like. He still hadn't provided that information to the police. There was no paper trail from the plastic surgery he'd done years ago to hide the man's real identity. All that had been destroyed, if it ever existed in the first place.

Their only shot—aside from getting someone close to the kingpin to betray him—was buried in George Anderson's memory. And he wasn't talking.

Yet.

Jasper stepped out. George Anderson came up behind him. "I'm not staying here."

Jasper's instincts were all firing.

What was going on?

Something was not right here. Things were too quiet and it was setting his nerves on edge. "Hang on." Better to be cautious than to get them moving and end up with a disaster.

A bullet slammed into Jasper's vest. Then another shot zipped past him. And several more. Who knew how many. He stumbled back, slammed into George, and the two of them tumbled into the house. Gage and Blake were yelling. Jasper could only hear a rush in his ears.

He tried to breathe.

Fire burst in his chest. *I've been shot.*

He stared down at the bullet embedded in the front of his vest. Spots flashed before his eyes. He leaned his head back, and it hit the floor.

"Shots fired! Shots fired!"

"Officer down!"

Jasper closed his eyes. As if doing so could cut down some of the noise and stop his head pounding. He got his hands around his weapon. Lifted his shoulders and looked out the door, gun up barely half a foot off his body.

Breathed.

Someone moved behind him. Jasper twisted around— which hurt enough he cried out. George Anderson lay on the ground. An officer dragged him out from under Jasper, streaking blood across the floor.

Jasper tried to say, "Ambulance."

"On the way." The officer kept his head low while behind him the other three held the cuffed gangbangers in place in the hallway. "Stay where you are."

Jasper didn't like that idea.

Gage and Blake came back into the entryway. Blake asked, "George?"

Good question. Gage grabbed the sides of Jasper's vest and hauled him up to sit with his back to the wall and said, "Tuck your feet. EMTs need to get to George."

Jasper caught his eyes before they rolled back in his head. "Destiny." He needed to call her. She and Clare would find out through the grapevine that a cop had been shot. They'd wonder if it was Gage or Blake—or him.

Gage knelt in front of him, checking the spot where the bullet had hit his vest. "You're gonna have a huge bruise."

"Least it didn't hit my face." His head swam.

"Yeah, wouldn't want to ruin that face." Gage patted his cheek with a gloved hand, more relief in his expression than Jasper had been expecting.

His eyes started to roll back again. *Nope, don't pass out.* He blinked. George had the same entryway light fixture they'd had when he was little. He and Caleb had lain on the floor together and watched the Christmas lights from the tree reflect across the ceiling and hit the pieces of glass.

"Who is Caleb?" Gage asked.

Apparently, he'd spoken aloud.

Jasper said, "He was my brother." Tears filled his eyes. Why did his chest hurt this bad? He could barely breathe. "He died." Jasper could feel it coming. "I'm gonna pass out now."

Before he did, he saw a different expression on Gage's face. One that looked a whole lot like compassion. And respect.

TWENTY

"I should talk to a hospital administrator." The automatic doors opened in front of them, and Clare continued, "Find out if they have some kind of frequent flyer plan."

Neither of them smiled. Destiny just wanted to see Jasper for herself so she would know that he really was all right. He'd texted her on the drive over, and she'd nearly passed out she was so relieved. After hearing the "officer down" call had gone out, she hadn't known what to think.

She slid her phone into her back pocket now. Her winter jacket was getting tight around her middle, so she left it open. The shirt she wore was loose. After Africa, she'd avoided tight-fitting clothing anyway, but it would get harder and harder to disguise her condition.

Gage and Blake stood in the waiting area with half a dozen uniformed cops—including some higher-ranking officers. Violet stood beside Blake.

Destiny headed for her future sister-in-law and gave her a hug. "How is your father?"

Violet worried her lip between her teeth. "He's in surgery. It hit his shoulder."

"Like Jasper's mother?" That was weird, wasn't it?

Gage said, "Same exact spot. As though on purpose."

"Far too close to be a coincidence," her brother said. "So, we have to believe it was intentional."

"Like he was trying to kill them, and the bullet went just a little high of where he aimed?" she asked.

Clare shook her head, leaning against Gage. Probably overwhelmed with relief that her husband was unharmed. "He would have corrected after the cemetery."

Blake said, "And your Famous Ones haven't found him yet?" There was an insinuation in his tone.

"They'll check in." Why did Destiny feel the need to defend them? Except for the obvious. "I owe them my life, you know."

Blake made a face. "I know. But this shooter is a menace."

Added to the issue with Brent Rammington and the victims piling up and whatever the kingpin was doing, this shooter was one more thing they didn't need.

"Aren't you going to ask about Jasper?" Blake stared at her.

She waved her phone. "He said he's fine. But I would like to see him. Where is he?"

Her brother blinked, then grudgingly said, "Down the hall on the right."

So that it didn't look like she was running down there to get a look at him, she said, "Is his mother still here? I might check on her also."

Gage said, "The doctor told me she wasn't having visitors. I think the senator had to go back to work, so he isn't here."

"Okay, thanks." She was doing pretty good at staying cool.

Not worrying about if she'd been the target. It wasn't like that made sense. Now Jasper had been shot? What was going on? Either a very skilled shooter was purposely missing or... She had no idea. Because she had been a waitress up until a few months ago. Following the Lord had brought her to being in the middle of this police investigation. Pregnant. Working for Vanguard.

She spotted him through the window, sitting on the side of the hospital bed with no shirt on. The bruise on his chest was huge. She yelped.

Jasper looked over. His expression softened, and he motioned for her, mouthing, *Come here.*

She slid the door open. "That looks like it *hurts.*" The door didn't want to close behind her. She looked and found Blake right behind her. *He wants to see this?* Okay. She went to Jasper and looked at the enormity of it. "Did it do more than surface damage?" She touched the edge, up by his collarbone.

Jasper laid his hand on hers. "No bone damage. Which is a miracle. Just this lovely bruise to remember a sweet time."

She didn't find it funny.

Blake said, "George got winged like your mother in the exact same spot. You saved his life. Now tell us about your brother that died."

Destiny frowned. She glanced between them. "They know about Caleb?"

Blake's brows rose. "*You* know about Caleb?"

She tried to tug her hand from under Jasper's, but he didn't let go. He lowered their hands but held on to hers. As though he needed the solidarity.

She said, "Oh, well, it was actually Richard who told me."

"The *senator?*"

Jasper said, "Bro." As if it was all that needed to be said.

Then, he cleared his throat. "Caleb had leukemia. I was eight when he died. He was seven."

Her brother paled. "You never said anything."

"It's not something I talk about."

Destiny said, "People are allowed to keep their own confidence if it's too painful to talk about. Or whenever they want."

"This isn't about you." Her brother looked at her like...

Destiny said, "I know I'm different since what happened in Africa." And he didn't know the whole of it. "But you don't have to look at me like that."

Jasper reached behind him, tugged on his T-shirt, and stood. Between Destiny and her brother. "She doesn't need to deal with your judgment."

"Yeah?" Blake asked. "What made you the guy that stands for her?"

Destiny couldn't see her brother. Jasper stood between them. If only she could hide here behind his back. Maybe forever. Not because she was scared of her brother. Just because it was Jasper, and being protected by him made her feel safer than she ever had in her life. He knew about the baby, so he wasn't just protecting her. He was protecting her and her child.

"What's going on?" Blake asked. "I'm not stupid, Des. Don't treat me like I am. You haven't been okay since you got back."

Jasper shifted, just enough that she could see her brother and he would still be able to intervene. As though he wanted to cover her, no matter what came.

"That's why I wanted a family meeting." She had to be able to say it out loud. She'd managed it with Jasper in the bathroom, but that was him. Her brother... She loved Blake, but he had his own ideas about what his sisters should do. Where they should go. Who they should be.

She did what she felt God led her to. But it would never be Blake's view of "ideal." Then again, while she'd been gone, he had become a Christian. So maybe God was changing her brother.

"Tell me." Blake's expression softened as much as it could.

She could end up driving a wedge between him and Jasper, and that was the last thing she wanted responsibility for. There was already enough on her plate. "I'm pregnant."

Blake's eyes narrowed, just a flex. He glanced at Jasper. Glanced at her. "You're...*what?*"

She tried to say it. Nothing came out. She had to breathe. Jasper tugged her into his side. His words blurred in her ears. She made a point not to lean against his chest, even though she wanted to more than anything. It would hurt him if she went anywhere near his bruise.

Blake's eyes filled with tears. "You should have told me."

"I was dealing with it." She cleared her throat. "Processing what it meant."

It was on the tip of her tongue to say, "I'm sorry," but she'd been told over and over the past few weeks that she had nothing to be sorry for, so she'd quit saying it as a reflex. Apparently, the Famous Ones' mantra had sunk in. *It wasn't my fault.*

They'd killed the girl she was kidnapped with and raped Destiny before she was rescued.

Double tragedy didn't mean she wouldn't suffer the rest of her life, but it also didn't beget a life of tragedy. Life was just life.

She said, "I'm doing okay." And it was true.

Blake tugged her close for a hug, and she held on to her

brother, even though she registered some kind of commotion in the hallway.

Jasper went to the door. At least, that was the conclusion she drew from what she heard with her eyes closed, standing in her brother's arms.

"I'm all right."

"You better be."

She rolled her eyes because big brothers were weird and annoying. "Will you help me tell Grace, Mercy, and Hope?"

He nodded against her hair. "Sure, kiddo. I'll help you with whatever you need." He pulled back. "Both Violet and I will. I know she'll be on board."

She didn't need to cry for the millionth time, but apparently, that didn't factor. Tears rolled down her cheeks. "Thanks."

Blake tugged her head against him again.

Out in the hallway, someone screamed, high-pitched. A woman. Destiny stepped around her brother, reluctantly separating from the support. She'd never been a hugger before. That was another thing different about her these days.

"What is..?" She didn't understand what she was looking at.

Jasper faced off with *his mother*? Hands raised. His mom wore a hospital gown, thankfully tied in the back. A bandage came up out of the collar on her left shoulder at the neckline. Her face was pale, and her eyes glassy and wild. Hair stringy and all over the place.

A security guard ran up behind her, red-faced and out of breath. "Mrs. Hollingsworth—"

She screamed like a banshee.

Jasper waved the guy off. "Don't." He took a step closer to her. "Mom, put the scalpel down."

"She's trying to kill all of us! I'm gonna end her before she kills you!"

TWENTY-ONE

"Mom, listen to me." As if his words would get through to her. When she was like this, there was nothing Jasper could say or do that would get her to listen. Not a thing even penetrated the fog in her mind—or the strength of what she had decided was true. "Elaine."

"She's trying to kill us!"

"Mom, Destiny doesn't even know you." Maybe that would get past her mental block. "She's never even met you."

"Just like that other one! She tried to kill me, and you did nothing!"

Jasper's chest thrummed with pain. The only time it hadn't hurt was when Destiny came in, and he'd been able to think about her instead of the injury. The feel of her hand on his chest. What pain he'd felt from being hit by a bullet to the vest had disappeared.

Now this?

It was proof there was no God in heaven. And if there was, then He certainly was no heavenly Father. Jasper knew what everyone thought of his dad, and how the senator acted.

The truth was he'd been as good of a father as he was capable of being. Even with their differences, he and his dad were a team.

They backed each other up because it took both of them to contend with the woman in front of him. Even if they were at odds over nearly everything else.

"You have to put the scalpel down, Mom." He could see the scars on her arms from the last time, and the time before that. "Nobody needs to get hurt."

"I'm already hurt!"

He winced. "I haven't forgotten."

"But you don't care! I nearly died, Caleb."

A lump rose in Jasper's throat. Behind her, he spotted a couple of orderlies from the psych ward. The one she wasn't supposed to have walked out of. She should have never reached the ER. Someone must have told her that he'd been hurt.

Still, her fractured mind believed him to be both Caleb and Jasper.

"You're here, and so am I. Both of us can work together to figure this out." He took another step toward her. "We can do it together, Mom."

The orderly behind her raised a needle. They wanted to give her a drug that would knock her out so she didn't hurt herself or anyone else.

He nodded, just slightly. "It's gonna be okay. But you must put the scalpel down."

Her eyes darted around, not really focusing. He could clearly remember times when she'd been lucid. When his mom had played with them or taken them to the park. A few years ago, during a good period, she'd started social programs and been on committees. Jasper never knew she had a drug problem. Around his fifteenth birthday, one wrong pill, cut with something dangerous, caused her mental functioning to change forever.

It was a miracle they'd been able to keep it out of the public eye, though plenty of people knew she was a recluse. Or some kind of kept woman. Not many people chose to look past their own opinions or conclusions.

The orderly wound an arm around her from behind. Jasper grasped her wrist, forcing her to drop the blade. She screamed. The needle was plunged into her neck. It took a few seconds, usually. At least they accounted for her shoulder injury.

"Thanks." He wanted to do this. "I've got her."

He lifted his mom into his arms and walked down the hall. Maybe it was so he could be the one who carried her back to her hospital bed, where she could get the care she needed. Or maybe it was so he didn't have to turn around and see all his friends behind him.

People he considered family. Even though they'd only just found out about Caleb.

It wasn't like he talked about his personal life all that much.

He and his father had learned to keep it tight and not let a lot of people in on the truth. The media had frenzied around Caleb's treatment, publicizing the failure of the doctors. Even though no one could've controlled the outcome. Not everyone who had leukemia survived. If he could understand why God allowed it to happen that way, he might be a step closer to thinking about faith in Him. Now that he knew the truth of what happened to Destiny?

It seemed like God didn't do much to help folks that trusted in Him.

Caleb had prayed.

He still died.

At least his brother was in heaven. If Jasper wanted to see him again, he'd have to make sure he went there as well. But there was still too much he couldn't reconcile. So much that it felt like a war constantly raging in his chest. The only thing that stilled the chaos was Destiny, but she didn't need the weight of being his anchor.

Jasper laid his mother on the bed, and her head lolled to the side. He brushed hair off her face.

"Listen, I'm sorry—"

He straightened, glancing through the resident doctor. "I don't wanna hear it. I want you to take care of her, not make excuses."

He sounded like an uppity rich guy, but the reality was that his mom could've easily hurt herself or someone else.

One day, she would. And he might not find her before it was too late. Or he might give in to the worst part of himself and believe it was better if he did nothing.

If he just let her go.

He walked out before the doctor—who was younger than him—could say anything else. His phone rang, but he silenced it through the material of his pocket, not even looking to see who was calling. It felt like his entire life had crashed, like multiple planes colliding in midair. He'd seen that tragic spectacle at an air show decades ago. One of his dad's attempts to distract both of them from Caleb being gone and his mother being in the hospital again.

Thankfully, no one had died. The pilots had all ejected in time. Still, watching it happen in front of him had been harrowing.

Not all that different from how it had felt to hear Destiny was a captive of dangerous men.

He trudged back down the hallway to the Emergency

department. Soon enough, he'd have to get back to work, but taking about three days off sounded better.

Destiny turned first. The look on her face made it all worth it. She hurried over. "Is your mom okay?"

He managed to nod.

Blake, Violet—who must have come back from seeing her father—Clare, and Gage gathered around them.

Jasper wanted to rub his chest, but that would be a bad idea. "How is your father?"

Violet said, "He'll be all right, but he doesn't like being back here where he got fired from, so he's complaining loudly about the quality going downhill."

Gage said, "So that was your mom."

Not a question.

Clare elbowed him. "Gage! We said we'd ease into it."

Jasper looked at his boots, feeling the tug of a smile on his lips. There was nothing funny about his mom's fragile mental health, but no one in this group was lying to anyone else anymore. It felt good that all the secrets were out.

They knew Destiny's condition.

The can of worms that was his mother had been opened.

They all knew now why he had a scrollwork C tattooed over his heart. So he could keep the memory of Caleb close.

Now they could move on.

Clare said, "Everyone, hold hands. We're going to pray for Elaine Hollingsworth that she can rest, heal, and get the care she needs."

Jasper couldn't let that pass without a question. "Does that help?" Maybe it only helped them to feel like they were doing something. "Does it actually change things?"

Gage said, "It can."

Destiny squeezed his hand. "When I pray, I do feel better

just doing it. But I've also seen circumstances change. I've seen people totally turn their lives around when they never would have been able to do it on their own. I've seen marriages restored. People healed of addictions. Medical miracles. Financial donations that meant a single mom could pay her rent. God does all kinds of things. And He even sent some crazy women to save me because they were 'in the neighborhood.'"

He loved that smile of hers. "I'd like to hear all about it."

She squeezed his hand again. Clare prayed.

Jasper closed his eyes because it seemed like that was what you were supposed to do. The case was out of control, more like multiple simultaneous investigations. His family was still a mess. His personal life was a mountain to climb. And there was barely time to think any of it through, so much was happening so fast.

But in the prayer, he did find something he had never felt before.

A whisper of peace in his soul made him wonder if there wasn't something to this Christianity thing after all.

Not just because it seemed like everyone in his life believed.

But because it might be true.

TWENTY-TWO

Two Famous Ones rode up front, and Clare and Destiny sat in the middle row of the black SUV. She hadn't asked if it was an armored vehicle, but they'd pulled out of the parking garage in the basement of the Vanguard building like they were the presidential detail. All to pay Brent Rammington a visit because he'd called and requested a meeting.

After two rounds of sniper shootings, no one was taking any chances.

It didn't matter that no one had died. *Yet* was the word the Famous Ones would use. Destiny just prayed and asked for protection. She thanked God that Jasper had been wearing a vest when he was shot right in the chest.

She'd lain awake half the night thinking about it...and the prayer and their conversation. How he'd looked when he had to go back to work and she and Clare had left. He probably worried over what she was thinking after learning the truth about his mom. A whole lot of yearning, which she had seen in his expression, like he'd wanted to stay with her. Like maybe he didn't want to leave her side right now.

Or ever.

"His wife is with him." Clare looked up from her phone. "Brent finally admitted he's trying to calm down his wife and convince her the blackmail video was a ruse."

The front passenger glanced at them. "Wanna turn back, boss?"

Clare said, "Let's keep our meeting. We might be able to help."

Not the first time Destiny had felt out of her element while working for Vanguard. Maybe that would never go away—and maybe it would always be the point. She didn't make assumptions or jump without asking questions. "Do we have any reason to believe we'll be targeted next?"

"Gage asked me the same question." Clare tipped her head to the side. "I think this might be the last house call I make."

Destiny wasn't sure she wanted to be the replacement in these meetings. As far as she'd seen, most of them could be emails. It was just that Vanguard clients wanted the personal touch. "If you let me know who you want to cover for you as CEO, I'll contact them, and we can start working together."

One of the Famous Ones snorted. There were only two, so if she threw a shoe, she'd have a fifty-fifty chance of hitting the one who laughed.

Destiny said, "What?"

Clare had an odd look on her face. "It's me that'll cover for the CEO job. My company, my responsibility."

"Okay, but—"

"Nope." Clare lifted a hand. "Why do you think I need an executive assistant who is responsible and picks things up quickly, that I can rely on one hundred fifty percent?"

"If we show up to this meeting with mascara all down our

faces, I'm going to tell them it was you." Destiny would start crying if she thought about what Clare had just said.

Her boss reached over and squeezed her knee. "It's not just because of what happened to you. Although, we might need a daycare in the building. Probably soon."

Destiny sniffed. Fine, she wiped a tear from the corner of her eye as well. "This is ridiculous."

"Maybe you've needed to cry for so long that now your body is able to release the emotion because you don't have a say. It's giving you what you need."

"A clogged-up nose?" Destiny could laugh about it, though. "I don't hate crying. My sisters do it plenty enough for all of us, so I haven't needed to that much."

"It's cathartic."

And Clare was the toughest person she knew. The woman had been in the army. Now she ran a company that kicked butt worldwide. Rescued people. Protected people.

The SUV pulled into a long drive. House on a hill. Secluded, set back from the street, and surrounded by tall evergreen trees.

"This is it?" Destiny glanced around. "Lot of places for a sniper to hide."

Getting out of the car might not be the best thing for any of them.

"Stay put. Both of you." The Famous Ones jumped out.

Destiny didn't like the idea anyone would be taking a bullet for her.

Clare reached over and squeezed Destiny's hand. "I could distract you by asking about Jasper."

Like how she wanted to marry him so he could be the father of her child? She mentally swatted away the thought. "I don't know what there is to say."

Clare snorted. "Sure. But it is amazing that he seems to be becoming more open to the Lord."

"And peeling back the layers for his friends." She loved that the guys he worked with were really getting to know him. As much as she'd been privileged to hear him talk about his brother and tell her what happened with Tessa. All anyone knew was that he'd broken it off when they were engaged. Painting him as a guy who tossed a woman aside because his family didn't approve.

In reality, it had been a much darker force. Now, they all knew of his mother's struggle with her mental health. The truth was far more than caving to his family. He had lost so much and then spent years trying to hold things together as best he could.

The door beside Destiny opened. "Let's go."

She got out first, content to be the test case for sniper fire.

"No one is going to shoot you."

Destiny shot her a look. "You hope."

"No one is gonna be that reckless with your well-being. Or Clare's. That's why all the Famous Ones are here."

"All of you?" She moved away from the cover of the door, and two women stepped out of the house, armed and standing guard. Destiny recognized both from Africa and felt a little better because she'd seen Tina kick that guy and break his jaw.

Amber had a mean uppercut. "The shooting ends. Now."

"Thank you."

One of them snorted. "As if you have to thank us."

She suppressed the urge to roll her eyes and settled on a smile, waiting for Clare to come around the car. "Girl, you look ready to have that baby."

Clare touched both palms to her belly. "One last appointment, then it's nothing but the couch and the remote until this baby comes."

Destiny nearly snorted—but she didn't want that tendency of theirs rubbing off on her. "As if you watch TV."

"I could watch TV."

One of their protectors cracked a laugh. "Sure, tell yourself that."

"I think I might binge *The Chosen* while I'm resting and after the baby comes."

Destiny gasped. "You haven't seen it yet?"

"Come over." Clare linked her hand through Destiny's. "We can watch it together."

They walked into Brent's house.

One of the Famous Ones said, "Dining room. Things are pretty frosty."

Brent looked like a shell of the man she'd met at his business. The stress of the last few days had taken a toll. He wore slacks with a T-shirt, and his hair had been ignored. His wife sat across from him wearing a peach dress and jewelry with perfect hair and makeup. Sabine Rammington clung to a glass of white wine like it was her lifeline. Her lips twisted as she glared at her husband before, during, and after each gulp.

Clare sat at the head of the table like a mediator.

Destiny stood beside her, not needing to sit yet.

"Explain that I'm telling the truth." Brent gave it a second, then looked at Clare. What he saw there made him say, "Please."

Clare turned to Mrs. Rammington. "Your husband was set up."

"He went into that hotel room with her."

"It was a honeytrap," Clare said. "They knew what buttons to push, and unfortunately, he succumbed."

"I was preyed on. Duped! But I figured it out in time to get out of there. So it only *looks* incriminating."

Sabine winced.

Clare said, "No one here needs to raise their voice. Regardless of their emotional state." She glanced at Sabine. "We have a sniper running around Benson, shooting people and putting them in the hospital."

"It's not like anyone died," Sabine snapped. "Unlike my marriage. My self-respect. Everyone will see what you did when that video gets out."

"It won't be released." Clare sounded certain enough that Vanguard must have taken care of the evidence. "But keeping it under wraps doesn't mean the rest can be swept under the rug. Someone targeted the two of you, and Brent has told us why he's vulnerable. There's a criminal kingpin somewhere out there with the goal of getting powerful people on his side."

Destiny caught what Clare was getting at. And it wasn't simply to stroke Sabine's ego. "Did he approach you and offer you anything to coerce your husband to follow orders, Sabine?"

She stiffened, then a split second later, downed the rest of her drink. "I'm dry. I need a refill."

One of the Famous Ones set a hand on her shoulder and pushed her back down into her seat. "Talk."

Brent asked, "What did you do?"

"I'll tell you *what I did*." Sabine straightened in her seat, squaring her shoulders like she was about to throw her empty glass at her husband's face. "I took care of my own business like you seem to be incapable of doing. That's *what I did*."

Destiny's brows rose.

Clare said, "They came at you first?"

Sabine glanced around.

Brent puffed a breath out between his lips. "And you had your father, or your brothers, take care of it."

"I'm capable of cleaning up a mess. Unlike some people."

"I'd ask for the details, but legally, I'd likely be informing the police."

Sabine glanced over at Clare. "Because you married a cop." Given her expression, that wasn't a good thing. "I don't need the police to fix my problems either." She got up and went to a sideboard where she opened a drawer, pulled out a manila envelope and tossed it on the table. "Neither am I going to fix yours. Sign those. I want a divorce."

Destiny flinched. Not what she'd been expecting to happen when they came here today.

Clare slid her chair back and stood.

Brent said, "You think it's that simple."

Sabine jerked a finger at the envelope. "It will be, or you'll get a visit from my brothers and my father."

Brent snatched the envelope from the table as he stood. "I need to speak with you ladies." He led them to the living room while the soon-to-be ex-wife poured the rest of the bottle into her glass. "I got a call." He hesitated. "I thought it was the blackmailer, but he made reference to the shootings that have been happening."

Clare asked, "What did he want?"

"It's not over." Brent ran a hand through his hair, looking far older in that moment.

Destiny's stomach clenched. Now was *not* the time to get sick.

Brent said, "There's a file in the Vanguard system?" Neither of them confirmed that statement. "He wants it copied to a drive, deleted from your system, and returned to him. He said to tell you to do it, or next time, he won't miss."

TWENTY-THREE

"Here." Jasper slid a photo across the table.

Gage picked it up between the ketchup and his empty coffee cup. Blake sat to his right. River was across the table, which was a bit awkward but not as bad as he'd thought it would be, considering the guy was married to Jasper's ex-fiancée.

"Wow. You guys looked alike." Gage passed the photo along.

One of the few pictures Jasper had of his brother. If only he had happy memories to talk about, but he couldn't think of any. "All I remember is the hospital. I don't have funny stories or jokes he told or much of any memories of him that don't center around him being sick." There should be some, but there weren't. Just that moment in the treehouse, a moment he probably couldn't recapture.

Caleb had been Jasper's best friend. And if he'd lived, they'd have had each other through all the years of his mom being better for a while. Then, she would fall off that proverbial wagon, and the truth of her condition would emerge.

He couldn't begrudge her the way she was or get bitter

about it. What would that solve? All it would do is rob him of the ability to show her compassion when she needed it most. They would both end up suffering.

"I never told you because it hurt too much to talk about." Jasper tilted his coffee cup and stared at the drip in the bottom. The eggs Benedict he'd eaten were the best in Benson, but now they sat in his stomach like a lead ball. "Caleb was mine, like a secret I needed to keep. Mostly because it was too painful that he isn't here."

Blake clapped him on the shoulder. "We all found a brotherhood in SWAT and with the PD. Whether we knew we needed it or not."

"That's right." River set his fork on his plate and wiped his mouth with a napkin. "We all needed to find something. Like Mitchell found me on the beach. Whether it's God or people—or both. We need that connection. We need to be accepted." His expression shifted slightly. "And Tessa would understand why you broke it off. If you tell her."

Jasper wasn't all that excited to dig up their history. "She's good, isn't she?" They were married. Maybe she didn't need that closure. "If she isn't, then you tell her. But maybe she doesn't need the weight of my mother's mental health or what I have to deal with. It wasn't for her to carry."

"So, you take the hit?" River asked.

Jasper shrugged. He'd always taken the hit, so why would he do anything differently this time? It changed nothing for him if Tessa knew that his mom had nearly killed herself over their engagement. Only if it helped her would it be worth it.

The server poured him more coffee, and he thanked her. He probably looked like he needed it.

"Can we talk now about how my sister is pregnant and neither of you told me?"

The edge in Blake's tone made Jasper lower his mug. "I only found out a day ago."

This whole breakfast was turning into a heavy morning, but it was long overdue as far as he could see. These guys had been in his life for years. If only Dakota could have come back from Last Chance County, where he'd gone for rehab and now worked in construction, and Liam could have taken a break from whatever federal case the taskforce was working.

Then the whole crew would be here.

But life changed. People moved on, created families the way Gage and Clare were doing—and soon River and Tessa. They'd pretty much all found religion as well. Jasper was open to the concept. More so now than even a week ago. Letting go of the rest of his frustration and anger couldn't be a bad thing. Especially if it gained him the peace Blake seemed to have even in the middle of learning his sister had suffered a serious trauma.

And Gage, at least, had known about the pregnancy for weeks.

"Thanks for throwing me under the bus," Gage said. "But Vanguard has their business, and being married to Clare doesn't give me carte blanche to know everything they have going on."

Jasper didn't envy the guy being Clare's sounding board and learning things that could potentially go against his oath to the police department. He could end up in the same sticky situation if things got serious between him and Destiny since she seemed to enjoy working so closely with Clare.

"My sister is my business."

Jasper had no female relatives besides his mother, but he could empathize. "They've been taking care of her, and as far as I can see, Vanguard has done a seriously good job at it.

She's happy. She suffered, but in the weeks since she's been back, Destiny seems to have settled."

Gage said, "You still need to talk to her. If you have it in you to be supportive, then she's going to need you to help her out. I'm terrified at the prospect of being a parent, and I'm not the one having a baby. Clare could go into labor at any moment, and she's out working? But it's what she needs to do. She's not built to stay home and sit around. She needs to know the company she poured her life into is running smoothly, so she'll be there. I'm not going to quit my job, either. That means we work it out."

"But my sister is doing this herself."

Jasper had seen Vanguard and how they operated. "She's not alone."

He would be there to help her as well, as often as she let him.

"Head's up." River motioned to the front door of the restaurant.

Two women stepped inside and scanned. One said something, and the door opened behind her. Clare came in between them, walking slowly. Destiny followed her while a handful of the Famous Ones tried to look like coming to a breakfast joint was normal for a bunch of women who looked like mercenaries.

Gage got up and gave her his seat.

"Thanks." She blew out a breath. "I feel kind of blah."

"That might have something to do with what we just learned." Destiny glanced at Jasper. Blake had beaten him to her and now had his arm around her shoulders. Jasper smiled at them, and she gave him a mischievous look for a second. Then she told them about Brent Rammington and what he'd said about their shooter.

Jasper scraped his chair back and stood. "We still have April in custody. We need to go talk to her."

April had planted that file in Vanguard's system. If she knew the shooter personally, they could find him and put a stop to this. He might even be the kingpin—or he could lead them to that guy.

"Conversation over, I guess." River pushed his chair in. "Back to work." He clapped Jasper on the shoulder.

Jasper wanted a moment with Destiny but didn't think he'd get it. At least not without her brother's arm around her and everyone listening. He settled on asking, "Everything good?"

He saw a whole lot of something more in her eyes. He would make sure they had a chance to talk later, about anything or nothing. Maybe cook her dinner and watch a movie on her couch. He could show her his house and walk around the lake behind it.

Except that would lead to thoughts about her pushing a stroller. Him holding a dog leash. Walking together, rings on their left hands. Living life the way they should.

Together.

Clare clasped her husband's wrist and scooted to the edge of the seat. He held her steady while she stood up and—

Everyone froze.

Gage said, "Not to state the obvious, considering what I'm looking at, but I think your water just broke, honey."

TWENTY-FOUR

"Where are you? GPS has you nowhere near the hospital."

Destiny grinned, headphones in and a laptop on her knees. The phone was on the seat beside her in the waiting area. She was off to the side so that Clare's close family and friends could occupy the main area, and there was less chance anyone would overhear sensitive Vanguard business. "The medical center where Clare is having her baby. It's private."

"Oh, wow." Simon's voice rang through her headphones. "Purliss Medical. Swanky. I'm on their website. Looks like a nice place."

"The receptionist offered everyone *Nespresso*. Took one look at me and asked if I wanted decaf."

"She knew that you're pregnant?"

Destiny rolled her eyes. Apparently word had gotten around. "I guess some people can just tell." But it wasn't too noticeable. Her stomach had barely started to get round. "Anyway, Clare told me in the car on the way over that I should take a tour while I'm here, meet the staff. She said if I want to have my baby here that I should tell her and Vanguard will pay for all of it."

"Wow."

"I know." Destiny let out a long breath. "You ever feel like your life changed, and you barely managed to keep up with how fast it happened?"

Simon's low chuckle came through the phone. "Uh, yeah. But then, some days, it's like I wake up and it feels like I've always been who I am now. Like the past belongs to someone else."

"That would be nice."

"Sorry."

Destiny said, "You don't have to apologize."

"Wanna talk about work?"

"Sure." She smiled. Across the room, his brother glanced over. "Peter's here."

"I know. Someone has to keep the office running."

Destiny shifted her knee and righted the laptop. "No one blames you for the fact we were hacked."

"Doesn't make it less my fault. Or less my responsibility."

"You realize I've said that about myself."

Simon asked, "You thought what happened was your fault? That's crazy."

Destiny had apparently hit a point where she could actually laugh at the irony. Maybe it was simply that today would be a good day. Gage and Clare were going to become parents. The secrets she'd held were out. Her family was closer than ever. Jasper...

She needed to call her sisters and hang out with them. But then, she might be putting them in danger.

There was a fine line between fear of what they'd say, having to be there while they processed it all, and the fear that someone could get hurt.

Jasper had been hurt. But he was fine.

Violet's father had undergone surgery because the bullet shattered his collarbone. But he would be fine also.

Now they just needed to catch the shooter.

She said, "Jasper went with Blake to the police department. They're going to talk to April, see if they can get her to tell us who the shooter is. If she hid the file and he wants it, they're going to be connected somehow."

"That's what I've been working on."

Of course, Simon would be in a spiral working out how April hacked so far into their network so fast, even with physical access, but if he was able to pull out of that hyperfocused state, that was a good sign. He was a great guy, whose brother Peter seemed better able to handle the setbacks he'd been faced with. Simon would figure it out, though. And when he did, the guy would be a force to be reckoned with. An operator in his own right—even if it was only from behind his computer.

She asked, "What have you got?"

"When April was here, we collected her DNA and her prints. We ran that through the system and got a much wider spread than just running her ID. Buried in the system, we found another identity the Benson PD doesn't even know about. It's a familial match for her DNA to a woman who spent thirty years in federal prison starting in the nineties. She recently passed away from cancer."

"A triggering event." April had experienced a major life change that had sharply altered the course of her life. "Who was the woman to her?"

"From the DNA profile, forensics concludes the woman was her mother."

"So, her mom died. Now she gets tangled up with this guy?"

"A man the PD is hunting," Simon said. "Either her mother's death set her against him and she's hiding his things in our system or she's working *with* him and this is all part of some larger game."

"Maybe they're also related."

"Could be her dad," Simon said. "That would make sense, at least. Or a father figure. A mentor."

Destiny didn't like the sound of that. She chewed on her lip. This woman seemed to have slipped through the cracks and wound up in the middle of a whole lot of trouble. If she'd been preyed upon, they'd need to figure out how to help her even while justice was served.

"Whichever it is," Destiny said, "she knows a whole lot more than she has said to anyone." Did they need to tell the police what they suspected? "If her dad is the shooter, then the Famous Ones need to double down on finding him, and we need to get the PD working with us on it."

"They won't like that."

Sure, the Famous Ones wanted to take care of things themselves. They didn't want the police to "get in the way." As far as Destiny was concerned… "They're big girls. They can handle it."

Simon chuckled. "You can tell them."

"Anything on who the guy is?" They had a sketch and a federal file with no name.

"I'm hesitant because I'm not done putting it together, but I've connected it to an Interpol file and a file the Canadians have. They ID'd him, but it's bogus, so I can't get to his original, authentic name to start putting together the full profile."

"What do you have?"

Simon said, "From what I'm piecing together, it looks like he might be a contract killer."

"What's the file, Simon?"

Peter glanced over, apparently hearing his brother's name. Like a radar of anything to do with his twin. He sat with Selena, who was on the phone with Clare's mother, giving her updates. She would be here soon enough.

Simon said, "She password protected it. And if I try to access it, and I get the password wrong, even once, the file explodes and takes our entire system with it. The whole thing will be dumped on the internet for all the world to see."

Destiny blew out a breath. Her phone chimed, a notification on the Vanguard system, which showed up on the phone like an app. She passed the request on to the relevant department who would send it to the closest team leader. "If that happens..."

"People will die."

They had operatives in the field all over the world. People who lived quiet lives in the safety that Vanguard provided them, in the form of clean identities or assumed identities kept secret from the company or family they had infiltrated. A particularly dangerous religious group just outside Calgary had been on their radar for a long time.

Too many lives would be at stake.

"So, we don't try to access it. But if she gives us the wrong password out of spite, it takes us with it." Destiny didn't like saying that any more than Simon probably liked hearing it. The guy was probably fuming. "It's safe where it is, right?"

"But if we leave it there, he's going to kill someone."

She wanted to have bravado, to stand up and face down this guy. Be strong. But none of them were bulletproof. Her new life meant she had far more responsibility. Not just for Vanguard but for her baby—both of their futures. Wishing for a life of love and laughter with Jasper didn't mean anything if they lived it drowning in grief.

They'd seen the accuracy with which he placed his shots.

It wasn't worth anyone's life.

God, we need Your wisdom. There were so many things to pray for, but it was also time to act. If God guided them, she would step forward with the confidence that He would see them through what happened next. Destiny had done that in going to Africa. So far it seemed to have cost her more than she gained, but when her baby came in a few months, maybe she would feel differently.

Which made her realize something.

As soon as Clare had her baby, she was going to want an update.

Destiny needed to have something to tell her. Like a plan. The PD was working on April and getting information from her. Vanguard could take a different angle.

She said, "We need a way to contact him. We can tell him we want to negotiate."

"Are you ready for that?"

"The Famous Ones are." Destiny would be counting on those women to save all their lives.

Simon said, "Huh. Looks like the PD came up empty. April was arraigned and released pending a court date."

"She's out on the street?"

"I'll track her down and send it to Jasper."

TWENTY-FIVE

April shivered, but at least she was alive, even if she was freezing. Benson on a weekday, downtown during working hours, meant traffic constantly flowing on both sides. The lunch rush of office workers lined up out the door of that café on the corner.

The one where the barista messed up her coffee order and didn't even care. When she'd explained the problem with nut flavoring—the one that would kill her—he'd poured her drink into the sink and refused to make her a new one. They'd never refunded her money, either.

As if she'd go there to beg for a sandwich despite the fact she was starving as well as freezing. She would rather die.

Except that felt far too much like a terrible fore-knowledge.

She'd ditched her phone and the jacket with the GPS tracker inside hours ago. No one could find her. As soon as she'd left the courthouse, she'd done what she needed to get gone. To be free. All she had to do was reach her gym locker. Everyone looking for her would assume she'd go home or to the electronics store where she worked.

No one knew about the gym. Or her motel room. Or the two other places she'd left caches. A flash drive here. The account number to a bank there.

April had so many secrets that even she had forgotten some of them.

For sure, no one could find her.

She used the front door of the gym and waved at the receptionist. Months ago, she'd come here and put her padlock on the unit she wanted to keep. Inside, she had ten thousand in cash, two changes of clothes, shoes, and an unregistered phone.

Once she'd cleaned it out, she could head to the bus station.

Get out of Benson.

Out of Washington.

Go somewhere warmer, like Vegas or even as far as Phoenix. Warm sounded good right about now. When the summer came, she could go northeast. Keep moving. Never log in online with her credentials. Never dip into the money she'd stashed.

Never pick up her cat from the place where she'd boarded him months ago.

Stupid cat. She never should've adopted him in the first place. She wasn't the kind of person who could love another being—whatever it was. She barely cared about that cat.

April felt the tear trace its way down her cheek.

She sniffed and swiped it gone, cleaning out her locker. Pulling on a hoodie so that she could cover her hair and try to get warm. Hopefully. Maybe it was a pipe dream that things would ever get better. But if she didn't try, she might as well be dead.

Back exit. Side street. She hadn't gone far before a car pulled up beside her. She glanced over, just slightly, enough to see if she recognized it. Beyond the edge of her hood, she saw the wheel stop spinning. Doors opened.

Run.

She made it two steps, and thick arms banded around her. He lifted her off her feet. She kicked against his shins and knees and screamed. Didn't matter who heard, maybe someone would help her.

He turned her to face another guy. Tape slammed over her mouth.

They tossed her in the trunk of the car and drove.

How long she rolled around the back in the dark, smelling foul odors embedded in the scratchy vehicle carpet, swirled around her awareness like wind she couldn't grab hold of.

The car stopped.

April's nostrils flared as she tried to breathe with tape over her mouth. Tears leaked from her eyes. It didn't matter. They could kill her, and it wouldn't change anything. She had nothing to tell them.

It was already done.

Vanguard would win, and there was nothing these guys—or their boss—could do about it.

The trunk opened; the light far too bright, so she had to squint against it. She swung up her leg, trying in vain to hit anything and defend herself somehow. Her leg was blocked, shooting pain up from her shin and numbing her foot. He reached in and hit her.

She heard a crackling sound, and every muscle in her body cramped at once, like being struck by lightning.

A stun gun.

She woke up sometime later, lying on a dirt floor, half aware of her surroundings. She was alone. Pain stole her next breath. Bile touched her tongue, but if she threw up with tape over her mouth, she would choke on it.

That wouldn't be her end, though.

She could feel it.

Blood. Warmth that seeped into the dirt under her. Lying in the dark, April shifted her bound hands to her body and touched her front. Her shirt had soaked through, and blood coated her fingers. It smelled metallic in a room full of the odor of fresh earth...and something rotten.

She cried into the dark. A tiny niggling voice told her to pray, but she never had before. At the last moment of her life, it would seem like a betrayal of all she'd lived for to go back on it now. Try one last shot at redemption on the off chance it might've been true, and she'd been wrong this whole time.

She lay there all alone until there was no life left in her. No warmth.

Nothing but black.

TWENTY-SIX

Jasper jumped out of the passenger's side onto the sidewalk. Behind where Blake had parked on this residential street. Detective Jesse pulled up in her car.

She strode over to the two of them at the back of Blake's department car. "Tell me what this is."

"We've been searching for April for hours since we found out she was arraigned and released pending her trial." Jasper couldn't believe they'd missed her by hours.

Her home had turned up nothing. Her phone had no signal that Simon could trace, which meant she'd turned it off or it had run out of battery. Searching had gained them nothing.

"No sign of her?" Samantha asked.

Jasper stomped some feeling into one foot, then the other, just so his blood didn't pool in his feet. "Someone called the PD anonymously. They couldn't trace the call, and the person used a voice modulator, so there's no way for them to figure out who it is. Said we'd find her in this house." He pointed down the street. "Fifty-two sixty-four. It's the cream and tan one."

Samantha said, "I'll get my vest."

She started to turn away, and Blake said, "This is a trap. Why are we even entertaining that April is actually in here when someone just handed us the information?"

"You're wondering why we haven't been shot at by our sniper yet?" Jasper glanced over at his friend. Was he genuinely worried? Blake hadn't said anything. The Famous Ones were on guard at the medical center where Clare was in labor. "Why don't you check if there's an update from Violet?"

They both wanted to know the second there was news from Clare and Gage. Jasper needed to make the world safe for that brand-new baby. He didn't need to sit in the waiting room and do nothing while they waited for news when he could be out here working the streets and tracking down bad guys. Letting justice do its thing because of the work he did.

Better than worrying about a sniper—or the holding pattern he was in with Destiny.

Blake shook his head, phone in his hand. "No baby yet. But no updates that anything went wrong either."

Samantha had an odd look on her face as she wrestled into her vest. "These things take time. Could be it's over in an hour, and it could be late tonight or even tomorrow." She tried to shrug it off, but that didn't really work. "You never know how it's going to work out."

That wasn't entirely reassuring to hear. He clapped Blake on the shoulder, glad to be able to return the favor with his brother and be a support. "They'll be good. And Violet will tell you as soon as she knows something."

Blake nodded. "Let's go check out that house. What about the drone?"

Jasper wasn't sure about breaking rules. "SWAT gear on a non-SWAT callout?"

"We could bring in the rest of the team and an interim commander, since Gage is busy becoming a father."

"Let's check it out first," Jasper said. "Gear up. But this is recon only until the Intelligence sergeant gets that search warrant." If someone inside needed their help, things would change direction quickly. It was best to do this above board, which meant the paperwork had to be in order.

They approached the house with caution, Jasper in the lead. Single level, no car in the driveway that ran down the side of the house. A garage at the back had a busted door, so it hung down on one side. Rain or snow would get in above the door to wet whatever was inside the structure.

Samantha said, "I've got front windows."

"Copy that." Jasper went to the door on the driveway side. A kitchen entrance, concrete step. Newer lock, but it wouldn't take much strength to bust the frame and get inside. He walked to the back corner and looked at the yard. Weeds, and overgrown grass. A car tire with worn-down tread.

"Front is clear," Blake said as he and Samantha came up from behind. "Can't see anything through the windows. It's all cloudy glass and yellow blinds."

"Back door is open." Jasper strode to the patio with the two cracked plastic chairs, between which was a small table with an ashtray on it. Beyond the open door, he spotted a stained knife that had dripped a ring of blood on the counter. He pulled his gun. "Someone inside could be hurt."

"Right behind you."

Jasper stepped in, and they fanned out. "I'll take the bedrooms."

It didn't make sense that someone had sent them here. He strode down the hall, taking measured steps by instinct. Being a police officer was ingrained. Reacting with his gun between his hands, his finger down the barrel, felt more natural than putting on a suit and dress shoes and attending a party.

This was what he was supposed to do.

He opened the first door and cleared the room with Samantha right behind him.

She said, "Bathroom."

Jasper covered her.

He heard the shower curtain swipe open. "Nothing." She came back out. "Bathroom's clear."

"Guys!"

Jasper hit the doorway first with Samantha bringing up the rear. He needed to tell her how grateful he was to have her backing him up. She hadn't needed to come. April was her confidential informant, and she probably figured she'd messed up by getting suckered into the ploy about needing protection from her boyfriend. Maybe Samantha thought she needed to find the young woman to get answers of her own as to why she'd been played.

April might've been lying about all of it.

But why would she be hiding out here?

Jasper found Blake in another bedroom, standing by the closet where a hatch had been opened in the floor. "Crawl space?"

Blake said, "It goes deeper than that. And there are bodies down there. We need the crime scene unit."

Samantha said, "*Bodies?* As in, plural?" She didn't miss a beat while pulling out her phone. "I'll call it... I have no signal. You guys have bars?"

Jasper got out his phone. "Nope."

Blake turned his watch so he could see the face illuminated. "Nothing. What's going on?"

"Dead zone?"

Jasper said, "Or a jammer." He walked to the front door,

unlocked the handle and drew back the dead bolt. He grabbed the handle, but it didn't move. He tugged on it more. "What the..."

"You can't get out?" As soon as he shook his head, Samantha went to the back door. "This one is closed now. It won't open."

That was how they'd gotten in. He looked out a window. Someone was out there, and they'd hung around to lock them in the house.

"What is going on?" He tried the window latches, but they wouldn't move.

Jasper holstered his gun and pocketed his phone. He got a chair from by the dining table, gripped the legs, and slammed it against the window. The chair shattered, but the window didn't. He dropped the broken pieces. "The window is rein-forced glass!" He called it out loud enough Blake would hear since he'd gone into the other room.

His friend said, "In here, too. Everything is secured shut."

"And we have a basement of bodies?" Samantha's face paled. She took a second to absorb what was happening, then said, "Check every closet and cupboard. What do we have to work with?"

"A sledgehammer would be great." Jasper tried the hall bathroom. "One that isn't downstairs." He didn't want to look at what was down there if he didn't have to. Sure, it was part of his job, but there was plenty in his mind already that he'd rather forget.

Blake met him in the hall. "I shone my flashlight around down there. I didn't see weapons. Just dirt and bodies in different stages of decay. At least six." His expression did that shift he drew on when it was *bad*, turning his features placid. A defense mechanism. He would carry the load of what he'd seen, but he didn't need everyone to know how he felt about it. "We need to get out of here."

Jasper said, "Yes, we do."

"There are no weapons in this house," Samantha called from the kitchen. "The best I can come up with is to tip the fridge at one of the doors. But who knows how far they went to seal us in. There could be steel bars in the drywall."

They had to get out of—

Up high on the walls, white clouds puffed out of the vents. He heard the fan kick on somewhere in the house. What was coming out of the vents couldn't be good.

He called back, "A fan. An exhaust. Some kind of vent. We might not be able to get out, but maybe we can stretch a phone to get a signal. Call for help."

The smell of whatever was pumping through the vents in the walls hit his nose, and his body reacted even though he didn't know what it was. Not good.

"We need firefighters." Samantha pulled open the partition doors in the hallway. "No washer or dryer." She crouched. "Looks like the vent has been closed off."

"I'll check the other bedroom." Jasper took two steps, and the world swam around him. He slammed into the wall and stumbled to the floor. Pain sliced through his chest where he'd been hit with that bullet.

His head bounced off the rough carpet, and he passed out.

TWENTY-SEVEN

"Anything?" Destiny would keep asking until she got an answer.

Simon had found no sign of April, and it didn't seem like Jasper was making progress finding her. After all, he hadn't texted her back.

Things in the waiting room had shifted. People were talking less and pacing more. Destiny was trying to pray rather than get worried about why it was taking so long for Clare to have her baby. *They're fine, right?* She'd been in a nearly continuous conversation with the Lord for the last hour.

"Simon?"

"Huh." He paused. "Yeah, I'm here."

Rather than ask again what he'd found out, she asked, "How is the police hunt for April going?"

"That's what I'm looking at. The Intelligence sergeant requested a unit be dispatched to track down Blake, Jasper, and Samantha. Apparently, they haven't checked in and aren't responding to attempts to contact them."

"That's not good." She shifted in her seat to encourage

blood flow and to get rid of the itch to get up. "Don't their vehicles have GPS?"

"Yes, and from what I'm seeing, they're parked on a residential street on the south side of Benson. Which makes sense, with this…"

He'd hacked the police network? Or someone they knew had given him access to their computer system. Maybe it was a Vanguard perk.

Something else for Destiny to learn, but for now, she waited for Simon to figure out what he was looking at and pass her information.

Her phone started to blow up with texts from her sisters. Blake was supposed to meet them for lunch, and he'd never shown up. "My brother missed a lunch date."

Across the room, Violet was starting to look worried. Destiny got her attention and waved her over. Violet sat next to her. Peter came over as well.

She put the phone on speaker after she quickly explained what was going on. "Simon, tell me about that location."

If their cars were parked on the street, it could be any of the houses around them. They'd shown up there for a reason. Destiny needed to find out so she could understand what was going on.

Simon said, "Nothing on the houses around them. But down the street, there's an address registered to the company Brent Rammington made his blackmail payment to."

"That's the one." Peter frowned, settling into a seat beside Violet. "What else have you got on it?"

Simon said, "The sergeant reports someone called the PD anonymously and sent them to that house. They were doing recon to see if it was anything or just a prank of some kind. But they never called in, and it's been a while."

That sounded suspicious. "Something happened."

Peter said, "They were drawn there, maybe?"

Her phone rang with another call.

Peter said, "I'll get in touch with Simon. You hang up on him and answer that. But let's do it on the move. I wanna go to that house."

"Me, too." Violet stood. "We need a break, and they'll call with updates."

Destiny closed the lid of the laptop. Simon had hung up, so she answered the other call—from a number not in her contacts. "Destiny Reed."

"Hello, Destiny Reed."

She'd never heard that voice before. And it wasn't friendly. There was a sinister tone to it, as though he knew some kind of evil secret she definitely wasn't going to like. "Who is this?"

Peter and Violet turned to her. Violet took the laptop before it slipped out of her arms.

When he didn't answer, she asked again, "Who is this? Who's calling?" She couldn't make it sound light like a receptionist. Not right now.

"You have something of mine buried in your system."

She pressed her lips together. Less was more when talking with someone like this. Clare had made her take a training course online when she'd first started. Saying too much because she was nervous would be about the worst thing she could do.

She waved Peter and Violet to the door so they didn't distract anyone else, and they all stepped outside. She had to blink against the sun, but the air was crisp and made her wish for a jacket. Destiny spotted several Famous Ones operatives standing guard for their boss so she could have her baby without worry that they would be unsafe.

"I want it back. And you want your boyfriend back. And your brother. And that other lady cop."

When he said nothing more, Destiny asked, "That's it?" She put the call on speaker as she had done with the call to Simon. "I give you your file, and you release them?"

"I'll keep them alive. For now. But I want my file back." After about a second, he said, "I'll text you where I want it."

The call dropped.

"Let's go." Peter handed Violet the keys. "I'll tell them where we're going." He jogged to the nearest Famous One and had a short conversation while Destiny climbed into the back seat. By the time he got into the driver's seat, Violet had already leaned over and started the car. "They're staying. But they made me swear on my life to protect you."

Destiny smiled. "Guess we're stuck with each other."

Peter seemed to take it seriously, which she appreciated. He'd left his wife safe and was going out. Destiny needed to make sure her brother and Jasper and Samantha were all right. Violet had paramedic training, which might come in handy if there were injuries to treat.

Lord, don't let them die. I don't want to lose them.

She bit her lip.

"The text come through yet?" Violet shifted in her seat to face Destiny, who had buckled in behind Peter.

She looked at her phone. "Sorry."

Violet reached back and patted her knee. "It's all good. We deal with stress in our own way, and you have a baby to think about. I guess I was always meant to be a doctor because when I get anxious, I bark orders at people."

Destiny smiled at her nearly sister-in-law because Clare had mentioned encouraging Violet to go back to medical school. "I still think I freeze. So maybe I need someone to tell me what to do." They shared a smile.

Violet said, "You've got so much heart. You're the one that will make sure no one is alone or slips through the cracks. I might have everyone organized, but you care deeply. It got crushed, so it probably feels like caring would be too hard right now. But your soft heart will recover, and Vanguard will have someone to take care of people while the rest of us triage or kick doors in."

Destiny asked, "Have you thought about being a therapist?"

Violet laughed. "I'd be a better drill sergeant than a therapist, but I know what you mean. They're still doing those tribunals that I set up at the teen center to resolve problems."

"You might be a better big sister than me."

Violet said, "Or the girls need both of us, and it's balanced."

"Almost like God knew what He was doing when He brought you to Blake." Destiny squeezed Violet's hand. Then she looked at her phone. "Okay, we need to extract the file and put it on a flash drive. Simon will have to confirm we can do that with no damage to our system. Then we're supposed to do a handoff in the park."

She called Simon. As soon as he picked up, Destiny said, "Tell me about the house."

"You aren't gonna like it, but I've got work orders in the company files for reinforced windows, plus high security entrances and exits..."

Destiny frowned. "Why would that be on an electronic record?"

"Because people like to get paid," Peter said. "And money leaves a paper trail."

Simon said, "So if they're inside the house, it's a fortress."

"And they can't get out?" Violet asked. "Is that it?"

"I've already alerted the fire department, bomb squad, and rescue squad. If they're inside, we need to get them out."

Destiny asked, "And the file? Can we get it on a flash drive?"

"Just tell me when and where."

Peter said, "I'll be the one doing the handoff."

They hadn't even had that discussion, but it made sense. The caller hadn't given instructions on *who* should make the drop.

"I'll go with you," Simon said.

Why couldn't she be any other person than who she was. Then she would have answers. Or a way to fix this. Were Blake, Jasper, and Samantha all right? Would the fire department or the cops be able to get them free? If it cost them the file, what did they care? "We have no way to figure out what that file is, right?"

"Not without April."

Destiny wasn't sure the young woman was alive, though she couldn't be certain enough to be sure either way. Hopefully, she was wrong to assume the worst. "So, we don't know what it is or why he wants it."

Peter added, "Or if we're dealing with the kingpin or even if the caller was April's father, the contract killer."

"Neither of those men sound good." Violet glanced at her.

Destiny said, "The kingpin owns the house. But if the contract killer is connected to him, then maybe they're working together. Or the kingpin let him use the house to get what he wanted from us."

By luring police officers into a trap.

Lord, help us.

TWENTY-EIGHT

Jasper rolled over and groaned. He wasn't waking up in bed. He was in a house, lying on the floor. His chest hurt like crazy, tempting him to rub it, which would be a bad idea, considering the bruise. "Samantha! Blake!"

His friends were here. No cell signal, according to the screen on his phone.

Everything that'd happened rushed back. The reinforced doors and windows. Multiple victims in the basement. He had no intention of being another one on that list.

But it wasn't like he could survive just by being determined enough. *It doesn't work like that, does it?* Faith was a mystery to him. Blake had explained that the point was to give up control.

Could he do it? If it kept them alive, it was worth considering.

If he had to hedge his bets, the Almighty was more of a sure thing than his own ability to keep himself alive. Caleb had trusted God for the comfort of knowing he would be in heaven, but he'd also known he couldn't heal himself. Despite his desire to see his brother again after he died, to Jasper, it seemed like God didn't care one way or the other.

He'd have to figure out this entire thing. But that meant getting out of the house first.

Jasper pushed up to sitting. Blake and Samantha both lay on the floor nearby. He scooted down the hall and patted Samantha's cheek. He shook Blake's shoulder. "Time to wake up, sleepyheads."

Someone banged on a window.

Jasper got to his feet, but his arms and legs didn't seem to want to work. His whole body was sluggish. Whatever they'd been gassed with had sucked the energy and coordination from him. But why had he woken up? It must have stopped long enough the affects had worn off.

He leaned against the wall and saw someone in the kitchen window above the sink. A firefighter in a helmet. *Julio.* Captain Espinoza-Vasquez pounded on the window. "We got the gas off at the source. We're gonna get the door open."

Jasper gave him a thumbs-up and went back to the hall. While the fire department figured out how to get inside the house, he needed to make sure the three cops would be alive when they did gain access.

There was nothing to cover the vents with. No way to keep them from dying if more of that gas came out or if something more lethal had been hooked up to the HVAC system.

The system...

He went back to the kitchen, grasping the edge of the sink to keep him steady while his head swam from turning around so fast. Jasper slammed his hand on the glass. He spotted someone with a circular saw.

The world spun. He leaned back against the sink until he got his balance. *Okay, go.*

He set off, weaving across the kitchen. Blake had started to stir. Samantha lay there, unmoving. Jasper hit his knees between them, scanning his friend before he checked his partner's pulse. He could hear the equipment rev like an engine. Metal screamed against metal.

Jasper's head pounded from whatever they'd been gassed with. "Samantha." He rolled her to her back and felt again for her pulse. It was there but nearly too faint to feel. "We need to get her out of here."

"Ugh, my head." Blake touched his forehead. "What was in that gas?"

"Let's figure it out when we're out of here." He grabbed Samantha's arm and hoisted her over his shoulder. Jasper stood, leaning for just a second against the wall. Then, he gritted his teeth. "Let's go, Reed."

Blake groaned but levered himself to his feet. The three of them went to the kitchen where the firefighters still worked on the door. Sparks flew into the room. The spray made Jasper's attention focus on those tiny orange embers. *I'm not okay*.

The door flung open.

Captain Julio—Jasper couldn't comprehend that double-barrel last name right now—stormed in. The firefighters called him *Coda* but Jasper didn't know why. He just knew it was easier to comprehend right now than his full name.

Coda had fire in his eyes. "Samantha?"

Jasper rolled her into Julio's arms and the firefighter took his partner from him. The guy looked at her with entirely too much fear on his face. "Sammy." He jostled her in his arms. "I'm gonna get you out of here." Julio turned to the door and carried Samantha out.

"That's what I was doing."

One firefighter got ahold of Blake, and another grabbed

Jasper's arm and slung it over his shoulder. "Let's go, Hollingsworth."

Jasper felt the pull in the bruise on his chest and grunted.

"Ambulance."

"Probably." What had been in that gas?

Maybe it didn't matter. They were out of the house now, and the firefighter walked him down the side to the front yard where Blake sat on the grass.

A car door opened, and Destiny climbed out. In the ocean of cops, firefighters, and EMTs, he spotted Peter. Violet was with Blake, and they were kissing. Destiny set a laptop on the back seat of the car and came over.

He wasn't going to make her come to him.

Jasper got up. He ignored everything and everyone and made his way to her. Probably too fast, considering he sort of slammed into her. "Sorry."

She grasped his arms. He slid them around her waist and leaned down to tuck his face in her neck. He breathed in a scent that was pure Destiny and felt her chuckle. "I'm glad you're okay."

Her voice. So soft.

Jasper was probably a little loopy, but that didn't mean he wasn't in control. He slid his cheek along hers. But he might freak her out if he came on too strong, so he stopped. That put them nose to nose.

He was pretty sure someone snickered. Someone else was yelling, stressed out. It was all like white noise in his ears. "Hi."

Her eyes lit, and she smiled. "Hi yourself."

He touched his forehead to hers.

"Are you okay?"

"Just saying hi."

She chuckled in his arms. "So, you say hi to all the girls like this?"

"No, just you." He shifted and hugged her again, not wanting to let go. But they couldn't stay like this all day.

"That's my sister you're touching, bro."

Jasper turned to Blake. Violet grinned. "Both of you need to get on oxygen while we figure out what you were dosed with."

Destiny rubbed a hand between his shoulder blades, about the best thing he'd ever felt. He kept his arm across her shoulders. "Good idea," Jasper said. "Blake seems like he's confused about what's happening here."

Destiny shifted. "Maybe you should tell me as well." Her voice was barely a whisper.

He looked at her, their faces close again, but not as close as before. He tried to formulate something sweet. Something that didn't put too much pressure on her. So...a date? "Go out to dinner with me."

"That's probably a good start. But I might be busy tonight. We've got an operation going on."

Jasper spotted an ambulance pulling up and set off toward it with her still under his arm. "Tell me about it."

He learned why Peter was there and what he would be doing with the flash drive once Simon extracted the file. "What time?"

Destiny frowned. "You're out of the house and no longer in danger. So, we don't need to give him anything now. We beat the threat, and everyone is alive."

"Samantha."

"Your partner?" Destiny glanced around. "Over there."

He changed directions, and they went to the first ambulance. A group of firefighters had gathered around the stretcher. An EMT held a mask over her face, squeezing to push air into her lungs every second or so. Julio stood beside the bed, his mask off. His face haggard, and one hand holding Samantha's.

"Is she..." Jasper couldn't even finish the question.

The second EMT removed the stethoscope from his ears. "She's stable. Let's go."

They jumped into action, pushing the stretcher onto the ambulance. Julio helped push. One of the firefighters said, "You going with them, Cap?"

Julio shook his head, a whole lot of yearning on his face. "She doesn't want me there." He slammed the door shut and swiped his helmet on the ground. "Everyone back to work."

"Yes, Cap." The firefighters all dispersed.

Destiny squeezed his waist. "Let's get you seen."

"What was that about?" Something was going on between Samantha and Julio. Or it had, in the past.

"When she wakes up, you can ask her."

Jasper looked down at Destiny and spotted an odd red light on her shoulder. His brain clicked into a realization. *The sniper.*

He yelled, "Gun!"

Then he swept Destiny to the ground and covered her with his body.

A bullet cracked across the front yard.

TWENTY-NINE

Destiny blinked at the sky, trying to figure out how Jasper had moved so fast. He'd managed to be gentle about it, even.

Blake yelled, "Destiny!"

She turned her head in his direction. "I'm good!"

Above her, Jasper had put himself between her and any more bullets that might start flying. The police officers present scrambled for cover, organizing themselves into a search for the gunman. Calling for backup. Yelling orders around.

Blake and Jasper didn't go anywhere. The firefighters were rallying around them, and some were helping the EMTs to be safe.

Peter had his gun out but hadn't left their vicinity. As an operator, he probably wanted to chase the shooter with the cops. But his loyalty to Vanguard came before anything, and he'd promised the Famous Ones that he would protect her and Violet.

"We need to get out of here." The first time she said it, it was just a thought forming. Then she patted Jasper's arm and said it loud enough for Peter to hear. "We need to get out of here. To the car so that we can leave."

Maybe the tendency to freeze was, this time, a need to flee, but best to avoid a gunman firing bullets. There had been entirely enough of that in the last few days. Jasper had been shot. His mother and George Anderson were in the hospital.

Peter glanced over, a dark determination in his eyes. "Let's go." He tugged open the back door, stayed low, and pulled the driver's door open. "Violet, climb into the front from here. Blake, Jasper, and Destiny in the back. Keep your heads low."

Jasper grunted.

"You're hurt."

He ignored her obvious statement and stayed between her and the direction the shots had come from as they crawled over the sidewalk to the back door. Blake was already in, bent over with his face nearly between his knees.

Jasper climbed in behind her.

Peter hit the gas, and they weaved between emergency vehicles. Once he got them clear, he pressed the pedal again, saying a prayer aloud for anyone still in the line of fire.

Two streets away, he said, "Okay, we're clear."

"Amen." Destiny straightened, wincing at how it felt now to bend forward. Probably not something she'd be able to do for much longer. "Everyone okay?"

Violet turned in the front. "Blake, eyes to me."

He lifted up, slower than she had. Jasper stared forward, kind of loopy. A little like he had been since he came out of that house. "They've both been dosed with something serious."

"They might need a counteracting agent, or they might just need time."

"A shower and a cup of coffee." Jasper put his arm around her, reached over, and squeezed the back of Blake's neck.

Her brother waved him off and almost smacked her in the face. "I'm good."

Destiny said, "I won't be if you keep waving your arm around."

Violet smiled.

Peter asked, "Hospital?"

"Vanguard." Violet assessed Blake, feeling his pulse. "We have what I need."

Peter nodded. "Let's not allow them to operate heavy machinery for a day or so."

Destiny looked at Jasper, whose pupils were tiny. Her mind seemed to want to roll back through everything that had just happened, but what stuck out to her was Julio's reaction to Detective Jesse. "Did you have any idea that Samantha was connected to a firefighter?"

"Nope." Jasper overexaggerated the word.

"Feeling okay?"

"No." He stretched his arm across her shoulders again. "Hold me."

Violet snorted. Blake shot Jasper a dirty look.

Destiny laughed. "I think you might be fine."

Peter pulled into the parking level in the basement of the Vanguard building.

"I didn't even know this was back here." Jasper frowned. "Down here." He turned to Blake. "Did you?"

Her brother stared out the window. "There's a parking level?"

Peter pulled up in front of the elevator. "Let's go see what Simon has for us."

They piled in and rode up, getting out on the bullpen level. Destiny set her stuff down on an unoccupied desk and checked her phone. Now that Clare was in labor, it was probably *the* phone. Since she was in charge of notifications that came in.

She checked them, trying to keep on top of it.

Violet showed up with a can of clear, sugary soda. "Drink this. It'll settle your stomach." She clapped her hands. "SWAT with me."

Blake wrapped his arms around her. "Always."

Jasper leaned over to Destiny and kissed her cheek, bumping her slightly because his aim was a little off. Definitely, no heavy machinery for this guy. "I'll be back."

She glanced over. "I'll be counting on it."

They trailed off. Destiny sat with the can and her phone on the desk where she could see it. "Gage sent a text. The baby is a girl. Seven pounds, two ounces, and her name is Kara." She looked up and spotted Peter with an odd look on his face. "What?"

He cleared his throat. Simon spoke instead, saying, "Kara is Selena's mother's name. She served with Clare in the army and was killed in action."

Destiny felt the prick of tears in her eyes. "That's a beautiful tribute."

Peter seemed to collect himself before switching to a more pressing subject. "He knows we have his leverage. He didn't like that we got them out of the house, so he tried to shoot at us. We reacted too quickly, and no one was hurt. Now what?"

"Does the deal still happen?" Destiny asked. "We still have his file. He just doesn't have anything to force us to comply." She was new to all this.

Peter asked, "Can we contact him?"

"I could text back."

Simon turned in his chair. "I extracted the file, and I've

got it on a flash drive that's a little extra beefed up with security measures than normal."

Okay, whatever that meant. She said, "I'll tell him we can still make the exchange. I could play the new-girl card and pretend I'm overwhelmed by being in charge. Like I'm freaking out and reacting on emotion."

Simon said, "That could work. Make him think you're desperate to get rid of it before someone is killed."

She typed something out, and Peter confirmed.

After she hit send, she asked, "Any updates on other things?"

"All quiet at the medical center," Simon said. "The police at the scene you all just came from haven't found the shooter. I gave them the license plate, but no sign of his car either. They've got a city-wide BOLO out still, and it'll stay up until he's caught." Simon shifted in his seat. "I had to pass information about the house to the feds since they're investigating the financial side of Rammington-Harper."

"No worries."

Peter said, "They might want to take the multiple murders anyway."

"The...what?"

"Blake said they were in the basement. Including April."

Destiny didn't want anything to do with that, but it might be a reality of her new job. She knew what real fear felt like.

Peter pulled over a chair and sat. "There's no way we're going to let you get anywhere near that." Simon turned his chair beside his brother. The resemblance was strong between them, though she usually only saw the differences.

Peter said, "You're going to stay safe, and we're going to take care of things. That's what Vanguard does. We look after each other."

Destiny blew out a breath. Her phone chimed. "Thank

you." She read the text. "He wants to meet in the park on Merton at midnight. But he wants assurances I'll come alone."

"You wouldn't be alone even if it was just you." Peter lifted his chin, motioning to her in a way. "So, tell him you're the boss. You have people to make your exchanges for you."

She sent that as a reply, then read the response when it came in. "He wants assurances this isn't a scam."

"He wants the flash drive, but he has no leverage," Peter said. "Means he has no choice but to show up."

Simon said, "Tell him that if he double-crosses you or harms anyone, we will remotely erase the flash drive. He'll get nothing."

She typed out the text with a few modifications. She wanted to know what was on the drive. When the reply came in, she said, "Whoever goes can ask him what is on it. He'll comply."

"Good," Peter said. "And midnight gives some time for your boys to sober up."

Simon snorted.

Peter stood. "I'll go get the van ready."

"I'll come, too." Before he left, Simon said, "You're good?"

Destiny wasn't going to let on how their concern made her feel. "Thanks to you guys."

Simon gave her an odd look and followed his brother. Maybe they knew. Destiny decided to not care and went to find her "boys."

Things had gone okay today. So far, so good.

But how long would that last?

THIRTY

Jasper stretched his legs as much as he could in the Vanguard surveillance van and checked his watch. "Nearly go time."

Destiny sat by Simon. Jasper wasn't usually this antsy, but that gas had done a number on him. Thankfully, Violet hadn't insisted they go to the hospital and get checked out. He and Blake, not to mention everyone else, had spent enough time there lately.

He sat forward, elbows on his knees, and texted his dad. One heel bopped up and down on the floor. Too much adrenaline in his system.

"In position." Peter's voice came through the speakers since Jasper and Destiny didn't have headsets to listen in.

Simon wore one and said, "Copy that. Keep it tight."

Peter probably didn't need to be told that, but Simon wanted to remind his brother anyway. They all knew what they were doing. Why was he here again?

"Do you want to take a walk?"

He flinched. "Are you kicking me out?"

Destiny rolled her chair a couple of inches so her knee practically touched the side of his leg. "Are you okay?"

"I'm fine." He'd been saying it for hours. Since Violet gave him...whatever that was in an IV bag. He'd slept for half an hour nearly and downed half a pot of coffee since. Plus dinner. What more was there?

Destiny said, "You like being in the middle of the action?"

"I like being where you are." He watched that play on her face, enjoying the way her expression softened. She seemed to like him being sweet. Maybe every woman did, but her reaction was the only one he cared about. "You promised to have dinner with me."

"Pizza in the Vanguard break room doesn't count?"

Over her shoulder, Simon grinned.

Jasper ignored him. He leaned close and nudged Destiny's nose with his. "No, it doesn't."

She shifted slightly. Not a flinch, but not nothing. "There's a lot to talk about."

And he was making assumptions as to how those conversations were going to go. "Sorry." He sat back, rolling his shoulders. His dad had replied. He did the thumbprint thing to unlock the phone, then read the text. "My mom is staying put for a while. They're trying a new medication."

"That's good."

He shrugged. "She's been on a lot of things for a long time. What she needs is a place that will care for her the way a live-in nurse can't. Somewhere she feels comfortable." And wouldn't be able to hurt anyone.

Destiny touched his shoulder. Jasper turned his head, and she leaned over and kissed his cheek. "She'll be okay."

"Then why do I feel guilty just thinking about putting her permanently in some kind of home?"

"It's not like you'll lock her up somewhere scary." She

squeezed his arm. "You care about her, and you want to do what's best for her."

And a tiny part of him wanted to be free of her.

Free to make his own choices and do what he wanted with his life without worrying about if she'd try and kill herself again in reaction to it. If—or when—he got engaged again, there was no way he would tell her. But then, did that mean he'd live two separate lives and never tell her? He'd have to pretend for the rest of her life that he didn't have a family.

The one he'd always wanted.

Simon glanced over. "He's here."

Destiny turned to her spot, and Jasper shifted his chair over so he could watch the video feeds.

A man on-screen approached Peter.

Jasper whispered, "That's the guy from the sketch." The one the feds had been hunting. Nearly every lettered agency had a warrant out for the guy's arrest. Strange that they hadn't jumped on this since the events at the house. Vanguard had sent them the information that was related to their investigation into the kingpin.

Through the speakers, Peter's voice was clear and steady. "You're him?"

The man said, "You have my file?"

"I want your assurance no one else gets shot."

"Ever? In the whole world?" He chuckled like he had leverage and not just a need to get that flash drive from them. "Not in my power, I'm afraid."

"April is dead." Peter's voice had an even tone. "Not something I want to happen to one of my people." He paused. "Let me guess. She took this, so you killed her?" On the monitor, he waved the flash drive.

"Revenge? That's not how I operate."

Peter said, "So, your boss or whoever hired you took care of her?"

Jasper tracked with that well enough. A little tit for tat, like using the kingpin's murder house to get Vanguard to trade the flash drive? Made sense. A contract killer who worked all over wouldn't necessarily have local resources.

The killer shrugged. "She double-crossed me."

So he needed the flash drive because what was on it was sensitive, and he didn't want it getting out. Jasper would go hard at a guy like this in an interrogation room. But this wasn't his case.

Destiny shifted in her chair. Jasper felt like he was hyper attuned to her. Since he wasn't out of the van on this case, he didn't have much to focus on except her—and the lingering traces of that drug. He touched her shoulder and a strand of her jet-black hair. How long would it take to get to know all the ways she styled her hair, like the style from the Rammington-Harper event? And how she got it like this.

She glanced over, a curious look on her face.

Simon cleared his throat.

Jasper didn't much care. Except that he needed time to tell Destiny what he wanted. The situation with his mother shouldn't rob him of the ability to have a family. Maybe it would—but it *shouldn't*. Then again, life wasn't always fair to good people.

Guys like this contract killer got what they wanted.

The kingpin continued to operate.

Folks like Gage and Clare might run into medical bills or long-term lifechanging diagnoses rather than a healthy baby girl.

There weren't any guarantees unless the guarantee was that things would inevitably suck.

Destiny shifted again. Jasper forgot about Peter talking

and watched her move her hand close to him. He touched her fingers. Held her hand. Maybe she needed support right now, or maybe she just wanted to hold his hand. Or she thought he needed that anchor—which would always be true. There might never be a time when she didn't want someone to hold her up.

He was all for a person standing on their own two feet, but everyone needed acceptance and support.

"Whoa, what's this?" Simon leaned forward in his chair.

"FBI!"

"Hands up! Federal agents!"

The view on the monitor filled with feds, people swarmed around Peter and the contract killer.

One said, "Hands up. You're under arrest."

Jasper opened the back of the van. Destiny came with him. She grabbed his hand, and they ran to the clearing where Peter had met the contract killer.

He spotted Stella Davis, one of the FBI agents from the Benson satellite office. A tiny detachment that worked in conjunction with a field office an hour away. "What's going on?"

Stella turned, her brows raised. She was married to Eric Hummet, a Benson detective, and she looked at him like he should already know the answer to that question. "I'm in the process of arresting the subject of an ongoing investigation, a man with multiple federal warrants. And you?" She waved a hand like this was a casual chat.

His mind scrambled for a split second, but he was holding hands with a beautiful woman, so maybe it was a no-brainer. "Just out walking with my girl."

Her eyes narrowed. "Right." She glanced around. "Surveillance van?"

Two agents cuffed the contract killer. Stella walked over

to Peter, took the flash drive out of his hand, and tucked it into her pocket. Then she tugged his arms behind his back. "You're under arrest also. I'm sure you have many interesting things to tell me about your operation and how you know this guy."

Destiny started to object.

Jasper squeezed her hand, and she closed her mouth.

Peter said nothing. Stella walked him past them, toward the exit. He winked at Destiny.

Stella said, "I'd love to know all about Vanguard's involvement in this. And how the PD got tangled up, apart from Jasper's dating life. That I don't want to hear about."

Destiny leaned over and whispered, "Can they do that?"

"They just did," Jasper said. "Vanguard has a lawyer, right? Peter has a right to counsel."

"It's in the phone."

"Let's go." The quicker they got back to the van, the quicker they could figure this out. Jasper and Destiny walked back over and found the van doors open. "Did we leave it like that?"

"Where's Simon?"

Jasper looked around. "Maybe he went after Peter?"

"He would never leave it like this."

Doors open. All their equipment just sitting here. "Where is..." He climbed in and spotted blood on the edge of the desk. "Something happened to him." And the screen had been locked. Simon had enough time to secure his terminal? "He knew it was coming." Jasper turned the monitor so she could see the scrolling words.

I've been kidnapped.

THIRTY-ONE

Jasper drove the surveillance van, the hard set of his jaw mirroring her own tension. He pulled up outside the medical center, and the front door opened before Destiny even got out. Which made her stomach roil. Two of the Famous Ones stepped onto the sidewalk in front of the fancy doctor's office and scanned the parking lot. Covering her.

She pushed open the passenger's door and hopped down. "He's been gone half an hour already." She'd been trying to hold it together and not freak out. Having Jasper with her, a pro at this and a guy who knew how to keep things tight, she didn't want to look like a waitress who didn't know what she was doing.

Then again, as a waitress, she'd tackled some pretty irate customers in her time, people whose actions caused her to muster up all the self-control she had in order to politely explain where they could shove their opinions. And then she'd pray for them.

"How do we find him?" She wrung her hands together.

The two Famous Ones strode over. Destiny held out her

hands, and a Famous One clasped her forearms. She needed that. Just a minute to anchor herself to something physical.

Jasper rounded the back of the van. "We should go inside."

Destiny wanted to run, but she stayed where she was.

The woman closest to Jasper said, "I thought the shooter was arrested."

"He was," Jasper said. "But I don't like being out here."

He lifted his chin. Some silent communication the operators in front of Destiny understood.

"When we get inside, someone is going to tell me how we get Simon back." She sounded like a bitter shrew, but that was better than freaking out.

She moved so they would all do the same. Someone opened the door for her, and she blindly walked inside. The ocean of Vanguard employees filled the waiting area.

At the back, a receptionist for the doctor's office said, "Now will you all go to the conference room?"

"Come on."

Destiny didn't know who said that, but she went with the flow. Sentiments floated toward her, people who meant well and probably thought she was in over her head. She spotted Gage in the hallway, looking worried. He didn't need to be concerned about this. He only needed to focus on his wife and their new baby.

She waved him off, and the flow of people entered a room not nearly big enough for all of them. "Why is everyone here?"

"You put out the call, right?" Jasper squeezed her shoulder.

Destiny frowned. "The phone alert?"

She hadn't known this many people would respond. A

guy on the far end of the room, whose name she couldn't remember, said, "Where are we at?"

Destiny said, "The camera we have in the surveillance van shows Simon was held at gunpoint and dragged out of the van. They wore masks and had weapons. One shot into the van, just a warning."

"But it wasn't the contract killer. He was being arrested at the time," one of the Famous Ones said, her butt in a fancy office chair and her boots on the table stacked one on top of the other. "So, it was someone else. My guess? The kingpin y'all are looking for."

"Why would he take Simon?" Destiny had to ask, even though it would make her look like she had no idea what she was doing. The Vanguard staff would realize quickly that she wasn't qualified for this job. She might just have opened her mouth and dispelled all doubt about her abilities—and Clare's choice of putting her in this position.

She could undermine Clare's authority and fracture the team her boss had built in one night rather than in the weeks she was on maternity leave.

"We don't know," the Famous One said. "But given his expertise, you don't kidnap a guy like Simon for leverage. You do it because you want him to hack something."

Destiny blew out a breath. She turned to one of the guys from Cold Cases. Bob Davis was the FBI agent Stella's father. But that wasn't why she gave the older man this assignment. "Go by the PD. Make sure Peter has counsel. Make sure he's not being railroaded by the cops. Find out what's happening."

"I'll get the kid back." Bob nodded. "You want him to know about his brother?"

Was he really asking her if she wanted him to lie to Peter? "Tell him what happened." Peter would be able to pray for his twin. And if he could sense his brother's emotional state like some twins could, then maybe he already was. "He needs to know."

Bob's expression shifted, and she spotted an edge of pride. He squeezed her shoulder and headed out.

Destiny blew out a breath. Fatigue was coming fast, but these people didn't need to know. Simon needed them all working to find him. She couldn't let them see that, in her mind, she was back in Africa at the mercy of—

The Famous One in front of her put her feet on the floor and turned the chair to face her.

"We need to find him." She had no other instructions to give them. "You know how to do your jobs. I know how to pray. Between those two things, I'm trusting we'll get him back in one piece."

She spotted Jasper's smile out of the corner of her eye but didn't look over. No one needed to know how tenuous her thread was.

"On it."

"Sure thing."

"You got it, boss."

They filed out. A few patted her shoulder. Destiny's hold on her sanity got thinner and thinner as more people passed her. She gripped the back of the nearest chair.

When the room was mostly empty, she squeezed her eyes shut and tried to push out the memories. She tried to not think about what Simon might be going through at the hands of vicious kidnappers. If they wanted him to hack something, then they wouldn't hurt him, right?

Another hand touched her shoulder.

Destiny flinched, spinning to face what came at her. Jasper lifted his hands.

"Give her a second." The Famous One passed him and headed out the door, closing it behind her.

Tears rolled down Destiny's face. She didn't swipe them away.

"You're breaking my heart." He touched his chest, right where he'd been shot.

"I'm not responsible for that!" She gasped. "I don't... I can't..."

Her mind spun so that she couldn't grasp a single thought. He would think she was weak. That she couldn't handle this job or her own recovery. That she would have this baby and fall apart.

And he would be right.

She was weak. Too weak for this. Too weak for all of it. She needed to be alone, where he wasn't watching. Expecting her to figure it out.

He took a step toward her.

Destiny held up both hands. "Don't touch me." She sobbed, trying to pray and finding no words, just a whole lot of fear and grief. She squeezed her eyes shut.

"Will you sit?"

Her body felt twice as heavy. He rotated a chair, and she slumped into it. Jasper sat near but not touching her.

If only she could put her head on her arms and cry until she fell asleep. "I don't know how to do this."

"I'm not sure that's true." His voice was soft.

So soft.

He got a handful of tissues from a box on the table.

She was a mess. He would wonder if she was like his mother, and whether he'd have to manage her outbursts forever. She didn't have the right to act like his mother. Their struggles were different.

"I can't tell you that we'll find him."

She pressed the ball of tissue to each eye.

"I can't promise everything will be okay." Jasper leaned

forward, elbows on his knees. "But I'll be here with you for all of it. Everyone on your team will do everything they possibly can to get him back."

"They're not my team."

He frowned. "No? That wasn't what I just saw. All those people who respect you, who let you lead them. They're here for you. The same way you're here for them."

"Is this a 'stronger together' pep talk?"

His lips curled up at the edges. "Only if it's about you and me. And your baby."

What did that mean?

"But we can talk about that when we get Simon back."

Destiny had to say, "Thank you." He'd been here for her. Things weren't okay, but he seemed to want to weather her storm, and she was grateful.

"I told you I wanted to stay, and I meant it."

She'd thought he meant at the penthouse when they'd hung out. Did he really mean longer? Maybe even...

Forever.

THIRTY-TWO

Jasper pulled into his driveway. Night had already fallen, but he'd had the outside lights on a timer since winter started. Destiny stirred in the passenger's seat and woke up.

She looked around. "I thought we were going to my place."

He'd said they were going "home," he just hadn't said whose home they were going to. "I thought you might want to be somewhere you can rest."

"I should be working."

"You can work from here." He pushed open his door. Maybe she was just grumpy when she woke up. Considering how he'd had her up on a pedestal for months—maybe years— it might be good for him to find a flaw in her. She was still amazing, but now she was a little more human.

He opened her door for her.

She climbed out. "Sorry."

Jasper chuckled. "It's a stressful situation."

Simon was still missing, and he and Destiny weren't out on the streets with the rest of Vanguard looking for him. The small lapping sound of tiny waves on the lake was a comfort he didn't know he'd needed.

"Doesn't mean I can take it out on you."

He unlocked the door and hit the light just inside, illuminating the laundry room that doubled as a mud room.

She didn't go in. "I've actually never been inside your house."

The one time she'd been here… He cleared his throat.

She groaned and stepped inside. "I kind of hoped you'd forgotten that I reacted to your breakup with Tessa that way."

By getting tipsy and having a girlfriend, or her sister, drive her all the way up here so she could ambush-kiss him on his doorstep? No way would he forget that. "It was a…good distraction?"

"You had just broken up with your fiancée!"

He grinned and headed to the coffeepot, trying to remember if he had any decaf…or tea. "Everyone hated me. My phone was blowing up with messages. Then, you showed up and…"

"I kissed the life out of you, all that righteous anger that you'd dumped Tessa swirling with how I felt about you. Being drunk at the time didn't help." She let out a long sigh and he heard her pull out a chair at his table.

Since he lived alone, the only person he ever heard do that was his father. When the guys came over, they hung out on the couch and watched a game.

"I'm glad you did." Jasper stared at the coffeepot. "I didn't need to be alone. Even if it was just a moment."

He didn't need to be having this sweet instant when Simon was who knew where, being held, being terrorized. Destiny had embraced the fear, processed it, and seemed to have set it aside, probably by praying. If he was going to hold on and not fall apart with worry for Simon, then maybe he should do the same.

What do You say, Lord? Think I can do this?

Caleb had believed. He'd talked about heaven right up until the end. But the idea had hurt too much to consider after he died. Now that Jasper knew exactly what Peter was going through, he had to trust that Vanguard had this handled.

It wasn't easy for him to give over that control to others. He'd been a cop for a long time, and a SWAT officer. Now he was a detective.

Getting shot in the chest and then doused with that gas meant he had to take a backseat on this one. But the feeling didn't quite leave. He turned, and she looked up from her phone.

He asked, "Anything new?"

"Bob talked to Peter. They prayed, and Bob passed on some ideas for how to find Simon." She checked the phone again. "I have a couple of operatives looking for Brent Rammington."

"Why Uncle Brent?"

Destiny shrugged. "Just a feeling. Like we should check on him." She shook her head. "Probably dumb, considering the shooter was arrested by the FBI, but I just feel like checking that he's all right."

"I'm sure he's fine." Jasper could call the man he'd considered his uncle, but if she had people going by his house, that was better. He sat across the corner from her and held out his hand. She set hers in it. "How are you feeling?"

"I just want to know that Simon is safe. Then I'll be okay."

Jasper rolled his shoulders. "Everyone is on it, right?"

"Everyone." Destiny's expression shifted.

He felt reassured knowing she was reassured. But maybe that was how relationships worked. That give and take, supporting each other. He didn't let go of her hand but would if she pulled back. "I'm glad you're here."

She looked around. "Your house is a mountain cabin."

"It's just how they built the place." His coffeepot started to trickle. "There was a couple who had custom built it, then he lost his job. I got it for a steal because they couldn't afford it. I felt bad, but my realtor said they divorced, and both moved out of state. In different directions. So, it's not like I stole someone's family home."

"And now you get to make it a family home." She blushed. "Someday."

Maybe sooner than she thought. "Thanks for coming up here with me."

"I was asleep. I think you might've hoodwinked me."

He grinned.

"You're sure you wouldn't rather be out on the streets?"

"Would you?" he asked her. "Because I can drive you around, but I don't like you being in danger. It's too risky."

"I can't be shut up where it's comfortable forever."

"But you can take care of yourself."

"Blake has already started in, asking me if I'm sure I want to live at Vanguard. Don't I want to have the girls around me. Don't I want Granny to help me." Destiny loved her family, but she probably also wanted to live her life. "Maybe that's part of why I didn't tell him, even though I know it's just because he cares. But he's still my big brother."

Jasper knew the guy well enough to know that was accurate. But Blake should know that Destiny could take care of this—and his friends should know *he* had this. Whatever she needed, Jasper was here. "So, we know what he wants. Tell me, what do you want?"

She looked at him then, and he saw so much yearning in

her eyes. Enough that it made him say what was in his heart rather than worrying about her reaction.

"Because I want to be the one that helps you, Destiny."

She glanced at their hands. "This baby shouldn't be your burden."

"What if it's a responsibility I would cherish?" He felt the same way about her.

"How is this, now, any different from when you and Tessa were—" She cut herself off, maybe realizing she'd implied that marriage was in the future.

"Tessa and I? We looked great on the surface. But she and I would never have meshed."

"You didn't want to live in the K-9 training center?"

"She wouldn't have stayed for anyone but River." Jasper knew that now. "And then I had to watch you leave for Africa. I knew if I said anything, you might have actually thought about staying."

She bit her lip. "Maybe that would've been for the best. Considering what happened."

"We never know what's going to happen or how our choices will pan out." He traced his thumb across the back of her hand. "But I do know that whatever is in front of you, I want to be there."

"Because you're in the market for an instant family?"

He leaned in a little. "Because it's *you*."

She closed the gap. Mostly. Jasper touched his lips to hers. Like the kiss they'd shared in Backdraft, it ignited quickly. Sweeping him up in all that she was, and now it was so much deeper. The strength and resilience he'd seen in her over the past few days only impressed him even more, and he had already been seriously impressed.

When he pulled back, he said, "You're amazing. You

know what to do, and you go for it. You follow the path, and you're certain."

Maybe she could be certain about him.

Jasper continued, "This life is far too short to hold anything back. I feel like I've missed so many opportunities. I don't want to miss another one just because, this time, the stakes are so much higher. I want you to know how I feel about you. And I've felt this way for a while now, Destiny."

She touched the back of his neck. Jasper leaned close again, and they kissed. He put all his wants and desires into it, the things he needed and what he knew he needed to give to her. The sweetest kind of exchange, and hopefully, one that would continue for the rest of their lives.

No matter what was in front of them, he wanted to face it side by side.

Together, as a family, with this baby and whatever children came.

The door opened. "Hey, son, I...ah, oops."

Jasper turned and saw his father in the doorway.

THIRTY-THREE

Heat flashed through Destiny.

Richard stepped inside and shut the door behind him, a grin on his face. "Well."

She pushed her chair back and stood. "Where's your bathroom?"

Jasper said, "Down the hall to the left." His face morphed from concern to irritation.

Destiny pulled back on her need to rush out and strolled instead. As if everything was fine, and she hadn't just been caught kissing a guy by his father. And a senator, no less! Although, she was currently overseeing Vanguard while the CEO was out.

Then again, Jasper and Richard never seemed to put much stock in their positions when they were in private. Jasper had every right to be proud of his achievements. He had accomplished a lot in his career, and yet he didn't throw that weight around.

Her stomach flipped a little. She needed to eat something, or she would get sick. Depending on what she ate, that might be inevitable. She locked the bathroom door and then texted Jasper.

> Can I have a sandwich?

His response consisted of a thumbs-up and a kissing emoji. *Guess we're good.* At least, them getting caught making out didn't seem to be cause to throw in the towel on the whole thing.

He'd really said he wanted to stick around. To her, that meant marriage. It meant being partners for life, and that was a huge commitment, one she wouldn't take lightly. Considering he'd broken things off with Tessa, he knew it was big as well.

The ramifications were bigger.

She knew people who'd married with one of them already having a child in tow. It wasn't impossible, just part of the rich tapestry of some people's lives. God was gracious, and He equipped people.

You're rationalizing it. But that was better than worrying or thinking up all the reasons it was a terrible idea. That could come later.

The fact was, she wanted it to work. With Jasper. And not because of the baby.

Destiny took care of some pressing business and splashed water on her face. She said yet another prayer for Simon, not wanting to lose even a second of asking for his safe return. "Bring him home, Lord."

She whispered the prayer into the quiet.

Her phone buzzed. The Famous Ones thread had far too many messages on it. They were about to quit looking for Simon and come find her, just so they would know she was okay.

Destiny held the button down to record a voice message. "I'm fine. You can see for yourselves that I'm at Jasper's. I'm good. Just find Simon, okay?"

She checked a couple more messages and found the latest. Everyone on the Vanguard network could check in from their phones, so she sent out a request for that. The FBI was about to raid the kingpin's house, and the contract killer they had arrested had ID'd the mastermind behind everything that had happened in Benson in the last few months.

A man responsible for so much loss of life.

He would be in cuffs soon, maybe even tonight.

She still wanted everyone to check in. It wasn't just the Famous Ones who worried about people they cared for. She even texted her brother and sisters, so they'd know she was all right and with Jasper.

Gage had sent a few pictures of the baby and confirmed everything was good at the medical center.

Destiny scrolled to Simon's status and stared at it for longer than was probably healthy.

Peter's check-in pinged.

She sent him a text.

> You were released?

He replied,

> Bob talked to Stella. They had no reason to hold me after I answered all their questions.

Destiny hearted the message as another one arrived from Peter.

> I'll find my brother.

She replied that she would do anything to help. He responded with a thumbs-up, and she prayed for favor for him. *Lord, we can't lose Simon.* Not just because he was an asset to the company with his wealth of skills but also because they all cared greatly about him.

It was past time to quit hiding in the bathroom. She trailed back down the hall and heard voices float toward her.

"She's your choice?"

Destiny's steps faltered.

Jasper said, "It's *my* choice. That's the point here."

Richard sighed. "Why do you always have to be difficult?"

"Why should it be easy? Life is difficult."

"And you'll make it harder doing this."

Jasper said, "It's a whole lot better than being alone and leaving Destiny to do this alone."

His words warmed her heart, but this whole situation was complicated. And she didn't like that they weren't aware she could hear them. It was a little too private of a topic for her to be eavesdropping. She coughed, gave it a second, and then emerged from the hall into the kitchen.

Jasper had a jar of mayonnaise in front of him, and he swiped a knife across a piece of bread. "Almost done, honey. You want cheese?"

It was on the tip of her tongue to make a joke, but she saw Richard's face. Instead of belligerence or some other frustrated emotion, what she saw was sorrow.

Over a sandwich?

She asked, "Everything okay?" and glanced between them.

Richard came over, holding his hand out. He took hers and said, "Welcome to the family."

"Oh, uh. Thank you."

Jasper grinned. When his father turned, the expression disappeared. "Dad, you want a sandwich?"

"Just coffee, thanks."

Jasper said, "It's decaf."

His father didn't look too happy about that.

Destiny said, "I got a notification." She told them about Peter being released and the contract killer identifying the kingpin. "The FBI are going to arrest him now, and hopefully, they will find Simon."

Jasper squeezed her shoulder. "I hope so, too."

"Who is it?" Richard had an odd look on his face. "Do you have that information?"

Jasper pushed a plated sandwich across the counter to her. "Dad, what do you know?" He faced his father.

Richard looked at her, then at his son. "I'll tell you what I know." He folded his arms, the coffee abandoned. "I went by that private medical facility to congratulate Gage. They have a sister center close by on the outskirts of Benson. It's a residential facility where they provide around-the-clock treatment for patients. I'm going to discuss it with your mother's doctor to see if that might be a good fit for her, long term."

"That's a good idea, Dad," Jasper said. "Mom needs to be somewhere she feels safe and she can be cared for."

"Things had been declining with the live-in nurse. So maybe this is for the best."

Jasper said, "Now tell me about the kingpin."

Richard turned to her. "You mentioned an FBI raid. Who are they after?"

Destiny swallowed the big bite of sandwich. "The contract killer identified him as Marcus Harper."

Jasper's eyes widened. "Uncle Brent's business partner?"

She hadn't put that together, but all Jasper's attention was on his father, so he didn't see her realize she'd missed that.

Richard said, "I had a feeling it might be one of them."

"You knew?" Jasper shrugged. "You should've told me."

"I only had a feeling. It's not like I'm going to sign up as your confidential informant, and I doubt a thought carries much weight, son." Richard had a point. "I have a lot going on. I thought taking down criminals was *your job*."

"You could have at least mentioned it. You were there at that event when his office was broken into."

"If he was being blackmailed, then he's hardly a criminal mastermind."

It was like watching tennis, glancing back and forth between them. When neither said any more, she offered an idea. "If he is the one behind it, then the FBI has to prove that, don't they? Everyone has the right to a fair trial. He'll get the chance to defend himself."

Jasper said, "She's right."

Destiny wiped her hands on the napkin Jasper had given her. "Richard, do you have reason to believe you're in danger?"

His expression turned immediately defensive. "Why would I?"

"Dad."

"Is that how you talk to your father?" Richard's tone dripped with haughtiness.

Jasper said, "If he's withholding information from the police that could be relevant to an investigation, yes."

Richard pushed out an audible sigh. "I wouldn't have come if I'd known you would be here, Destiny. I would never put you in danger."

"But you'd put me in danger and my house?" Jasper said. "There are safe houses you could've gone to."

Richard said, "I wanted to see my son. Is that a crime?"

"Depends." Jasper folded his arms.

Destiny was about to prompt Richard when he said, "Fine. I *might* have also been approached by this kingpin person. And Brent knew about it, but I don't think that makes him the one over this all. So don't go pinning it all on him. He just knew."

"Approached about what?"

Richard said, "Signing a state bill that would force Vanguard to close. It would break apart the business and dismantle it piece by piece." He turned to her. "Someone is trying to destroy the company you work for."

THIRTY-FOUR

Simon needed to stretch his legs. How long had they been driving around Benson, spying on everyone he knew or worked with—and his family.

Through the windshield, he'd watched Peter walk out of the police department with Bob Davis. Simon sat here, knowing he couldn't do anything to let his brother know he was all right. Their connection extended only to overwhelming emotions—anxiety, fear, or pain.

What was Peter feeling from him right now?

In the front seat, an older man, whom Simon had never met before, had turned far enough to stare at him. Simon's hands had been secured with plastic ties. His feet as well. One of his feet was numb, so even if he could get away, it likely wouldn't be far before he fell on his face.

Pretty much apropos for the day he'd had so far.

The guys on either side of him smelled like pot and had handguns tucked into their belts. The driver looked like he could lift a car and flip it over or snap the steering wheel of this SUV right off. Blacked out windows. Fancy enough that the outside had chrome detailing, but the dash screen had a crack in it, and there were fries under Simon's left Converse shoe.

The older man said, "Soon enough, they will make their move."

Like he had eyes in the PD, and maybe he did. That would make sense, considering how long he'd gone under the radar.

They drove maybe another half hour. Long enough for Simon's head to begin to droop. Adrenaline had dissipated until he realized he'd dozed off for a second. He heard a persistent buzz, but it wasn't his alarm clock. They were still in the SUV.

"Here they go."

One of the men beside Simon chuckled.

The older man turned his phone so Simon could see camera footage. The FBI kicking in what must be the man's front door. There was no audio, but the screen moved as a stream of people entered his house.

So that was why they had been mobile all day.

The kingpin took pleasure in watching the FBI find nothing in his house but empty rooms. Simon almost prayed the guy hadn't wired up any traps that would take lives, but why waste his breath?

Peter would be praying, and that was enough for both of them.

"Let's go." He nudged the driver, who headed for the freeway.

If Simon was anything other than himself, he'd swing his arms toward the guy on his right. Then, the one on his left. Break a nose. Knock them out, maybe. But if he tried it, he'd end up with another swollen eye to add to the one he already had.

Maybe these guys didn't know who he was.

Or they knew they shouldn't let him anywhere near a computer terminal, even to do some kind of task for them. At gunpoint. He'd still be able to fake a communication out, so they'd never know he'd given up his location.

But without a computer, there was zero chance of rescue.

What are they going to do with me? Eventually, he couldn't stay silent. "Are we just gonna drive around until we run out of gas?"

Someone snorted.

The older man studied him.

They'd proven to him that they knew all about his family, driving by where Lucas lived with Simon's sister, Freya. They'd driven by the house where Clare and Gage would take their baby home and the medical center—although they'd given it a wide berth since the Famous Ones were there. He'd have thought all that knowledge would mean he was valuable as an asset.

"I do have a job for you."

"Great," Simon said. "Get me to a computer. I'll do it, and you can let me go."

Back to his family and friends, his life. Why else show him everyone he cared about? Sure, he was vulnerable, but he wasn't the weak link here just because he was a computer guy not an operator. This guy didn't need to exercise his power and try to break Simon's will.

The older man smiled, but there was no humor in it. "This isn't a one-time deal. There will be no exchange or ransom. Vanguard might have employed you up till now, but that arrangement is no longer."

Simon asked, "And if I refuse?"

"Hopefully, you left things on good terms with your family. As it will be your final words. Your goodbye."

They were going to kill him.

The older man said, "You work for me now." He looked down at his phone and began to laugh.

Not good.

Simon was in serious trouble.

THIRTY-FIVE

"I don't like it."

Destiny leaned over and kissed his cheek. "I'll be fine."

In the back seat, his father cleared his throat. "I'll leave you guys to it." He climbed out of the car right in front of the medical center where Jasper had pulled up. The door shut.

Jasper said, "I still don't like it."

Destiny said, "If this kingpin person is trying to destroy Vanguard, then I need to talk to Clare."

"I know." He touched her cheek. "And I need to touch base with the PD. Or help Peter find his brother. But I'd rather hide with you and keep you safe."

She touched her lips to his. "Maybe when this is all over and this guy has been arrested and Simon is back home safe... we can spend a whole day where we have nothing to do but be lazy, watch movies, eat pizza that isn't going to give me heartburn, and not be scared for even one second."

"That sounds like a deal to me." As far as he was concerned, they could have a lifetime of those days. There were no guarantees, but he would do the best he could. "Be safe."

As if she wouldn't be? "I've got an army watching out for me."

They both knew that was at least better than leaving her in his house. Even though he loved the fact she was there. Jasper wanted to marry this woman. He would move into the penthouse at Vanguard with her if she wanted, but he would keep his house as a kind of vacation home.

She kissed him one more time. "What am I going to do with you?"

"Marry me, for starters."

She blinked, then chuckled. As if he wasn't serious. "I'll put that on my to-do list." She pushed the door open.

"You do that."

She glanced down at him. The Famous Ones came up behind her. Jasper gave her a look and took off. The door mostly closed. He had to open it and pull it all the way shut at the first light he came to.

Jasper called Blake.

"Reed."

"Where are you?"

"Where's my sister?"

Jasper said, "So that's how it's gonna be?"

Blake sighed. "I'm at the house watching the FBI raid. You need to get over here."

"What about Peter? Any sign of Simon?" Jasper told Blake what his father had said about the kingpin wanting to destroy Vanguard.

"Peter is with me. We think they might be holding Simon inside," Blake said. "I'll relay that about Vanguard. Peter will want to know."

"Text me the address." Jasper gripped the wheel. He

mapped the house and drove across town with lights and sirens on. Maybe it would feel a little like this every time he left Destiny and went to work. Every time he left her and had to take with him the knowledge that something could happen, and he wouldn't be there to protect her.

Did every husband, every prospective father feel this way?

When she'd left for Africa, he'd known she needed to do what she thought was right for her. He'd let her know how he felt and then said goodbye. Truth was, he should've told her long before that. They'd been dancing around each other for a while. He'd been too scared to take the leap, and it'd taken her leaving—and then getting seriously hurt—for some sense to get knocked into him.

He would always be a cop.

He would always be a son who wanted to take care of his mother.

But he wanted to be there for Destiny as well. To take those ingrained protective instincts and his loyalty and take care of her. Love her. Forever.

Jasper found Blake's car and pulled up behind it. He jogged over to where Peter and Blake stood on the curb, along with a couple of uniformed officers and more than one fire-fighter. "Julio."

The captain must have driven that truck with the red stripe and the decal here. On scene, in case they had need of bomb disposal, someone got trapped, or there was a fire.

"Hey, bro." Julio shook his hand.

Jasper asked, "How is Samantha?"

Julio's expression shifted. "She's your partner. How would I know?"

"Want me to find out?" As far as he knew, Samantha's

reaction to the gas had been worse, and she'd been admitted to the hospital overnight. Maybe she'd been released?

A muscle in Julio's jaw flexed. "Find out and text me."

Jasper turned to the others. "Where are we at?"

Peter said, "Once we get the all clear, we'll go in."

"No one has come out yet." Blake frowned. "I'm gonna go ask. They must've found something." He strode down the drive, and Peter followed him.

Jasper headed there as well, scanning around. He spotted an FBI agent off to one side going into a shed. He came out with a canister of natural gas. "Hey, Agent!" Jasper flashed his badge, a note of something in his gut.

The guy was one of the newer agents, a junior guy but older than Jasper. He couldn't remember what the guy's name was, but he hefted the gas can up onto his shoulder.

"What's the sitch here?" He nearly flinched. What a ridiculous way to say that. "You need a hand?"

"Sure. I've gotta take this around back." The guy made a face. "Stella's orders. Can't say no to the boss lady. I'm Veers."

Except she wasn't the usual supervisor, Addie Franklin was. But Addie had taken a few months off work for maternity leave, which left Stella in charge.

Jasper chuckled, walking alongside him. "Intelligence has a sergeant like that. Deerdan. Doesn't have the first clue what she's doing or how to lead a team."

He caught the shift.

The agent swung his leg up behind Jasper to knock him off his feet. Jasper whirled around and slammed a fist into the agent's gut. Veers threw the natural gas can at Jasper's head.

It caught the outside of his arm as he smacked it away. Not full. A full canister would've broken his wrist.

He tackled Veers to the ground. Jasper got a couple of

punches in. Veers' elbow clipped the side of his head. Jasper caught the guy with his legs, trying to pin him. Veers shoved up —right where Jasper had been hit with that bullet in the chest.

Pain exploded.

Jasper cried out. He heard boots pounding the concrete toward him. He blinked up at the sky and kicked with his legs. Jasper nearly blacked out, but he shoved the guy off balance.

Blake caught Veers. Peter, too. "Got him."

Jasper tried to sit up. His eyes rolled back in his head, but he kept himself from passing out. "What's going on?" He went to lie back on the ground.

Peter helped him up. "You good?"

"No. What's going on?" Jasper had trouble standing. That dang bullet and the gas had done a number on him.

"What did you do?" Blake shook the agent, now cuffed with his hands behind his back.

Peter said, "All the doors are locked."

Jasper turned to him. "Like at the murder house?"

"Yes." Peter folded his arms across his chest.

"Which means this guy is gonna tell us what's going on," Blake said. "Or I turn you over to a Vanguard operative who doesn't have to answer to internal affairs."

They dragged the guy back to the front, and Julio jogged over, along with a couple of officers and the other firefighter who'd shown up.

Peter said, "We need to get into the house."

Why hadn't anyone in there called for help? Why weren't they banging on the windows and yelling to the people outside? If they were trapped in there...if they'd been dosed with the same gas...

"We need to get in there *now*." Jasper turned to the front door, feeling as much fear for the people inside as he felt leaving Destiny. They were good people, the kind who worked every day to make Benson a better place to live.

A place where innocents didn't have to worry about a criminal kingpin.

Agent Veers said, "Might want to stand back." His tone was laced with amusement.

Jasper took two steps, and the house ignited. Windows blew out with a fireball. The door exploded, flung out, and nearly hit him. He flew back with the force of the blast. The door clipped his boot, turning his ankle an odd direction.

He slammed onto the ground, and everything went black.

THIRTY-SIX

Destiny had lost track of Richard a while back, after she'd seen him shaking hands with the guy who ran this entire fancy campus medical center. Evidently, it was more than one building, and they had a more remote residential building in the mountains.

Now that she had seen images of it, she knew that enrolling his wife in their program wasn't anything like locking her away in a scary facility. Mental health had come a long way. She might even feel like she was at a high-end resort.

The Famous Ones had been in and out, and they were texting her. She got the impression they wanted to be inside talking to her rather than on guard duty, but they were doing their job on a rotation. Allyson came in now and took the spot beside Destiny with a huge Frappuccino that looked yummy.

She eyed Destiny. "No caffeine for you."

"Don't remind me."

"Good, then let's talk about Jasper."

Destiny pressed her lips together. "There's a criminal mastermind in Benson trying to undermine Vanguard at a time when the company has never been more vulnerable, and you want to talk about *Jasper*?"

A couple of Vanguard staff members glanced over.

Most had gone back to the office after she'd told them what Richard had said. They were determined to shore things up, make sure everyone was good. Cover all the things Simon usually took care of, except that he'd been kidnapped by that same guy.

"You're spinning out." Allyson sipped her drink. "Calm down, honey."

"Did you just tell me to—"

Allyson chuckled. "Maybe you do need caffeine. It might calm you down."

"Simon is—"

"I've got some friends out looking for him." Sip.

"What friends—"

"They'll find him sooner or later. Plus, there's these *other* friends, and they can find him in different ways. Like online." Sip.

"You guys are insane."

Allyson smiled. "Thank you."

"That wasn't a compliment." Her phone buzzed. Multiple notifications showed up. Destiny scrolled through them. "EMS is pulling people out of the house they believe the kingpin owns."

"Marcus Harper?"

Destiny didn't have time to ask how she'd put that together. The Famous Ones had *ways*. They got the job done, and she didn't ask how because it was better to not know. "So far, they have only minor injuries. One broken leg. One concussion. The FBI's tactical team was in the house when it blew, but after they figured out they couldn't get out, they knew something was going to happen. They found the explosives, and their guy outside was trying to get a door or window open somehow."

"So, no one is dead? That's pretty good." Allyson slurped her drink. Her smart watch buzzed, and she looked at the screen. "Huh."

"Anything you wanna tell me?"

"Maybe later."

Destiny texted Jasper, praying he was all right, but also praying for everyone since it would be self-serving to just worry about him—or just him and her brother. She closed her eyes, holding her phone between her knees, and lifted them all up. She asked for protection, for safety, and for them to find Simon quickly.

When she lifted her head, Allyson said, "Amen." As if Destiny had prayed aloud.

The door opened, and Bob Davis came in, followed by Peter. Both of them sat in front of her. Peter had dirt smudged down the side of his face, and he looked a little rumpled.

"Update." She'd heard Clare say it like that, and it was time to sound like her. If only to reassure the people she worked with that she could do this.

Peter said, "I called Liam to see if his team can use their resources to find Simon. There was no one in the house the FBI raided."

Bob picked up where he stopped. "The team made entry, found themselves trapped, and the house cleaned out. They are all out now. And we have nothing."

"And Stella?"

"Concussion," Bob said. "She's all right. Mostly just mad they didn't find Harper."

"That's good. She'll be okay." Destiny glanced at Allyson. "Can we find Harper?"

"The FBI got their contract killer guy to tell them

where to find him. It landed them in a trap." Allyson paused. "He must've known that would happen. Apparently, this guy has these houses set up. Who knows how many there are?"

"That's not what I asked you."

Allyson shot her a proud grin. "I'm getting there." She chuckled a little. "Harper can be found, but he has to show his face first. He's gotta surface."

"Then why aren't we finding him?"

Peter said, "Between the FBI and Vanguard personnel, we've checked every house the shell corporation owns—the one Brent made that payment to."

"Okay," Destiny said. "So, we need to cast a wider net. Look at vehicles registered to them. Maybe an airplane. A boat docked on the coast. Overseas holdings. Vacation homes. We need to think like a kingpin."

Allyson had stilled. She stared at Destiny.

"What?"

She grabbed both sides of Destiny's face, planted a kiss on her forehead, and then ran out the door.

"I guess she had an idea." Destiny shook her head.

Bob Davis chuckled. "Yeah, I guess." The older man looked tired.

"You good? We are in a doctor's office. You could get checked out."

He glanced over at the reception desk and stood. "I might just do that, thanks. Keep me apprised?"

"Yes."

Peter said, "You can get checked out as well. Make sure everything is okay."

"I know." Having a checkup wasn't a bad idea. "I'm all right for now. What do you need?"

"I should go to Vanguard, get on Simon's terminal. See if

there's anything I can do." He stood. "It's better than sitting here doing nothing."

She understood as much, even if her role was more of a coordinator. Even if she wanted to be with Jasper at his house, looking at the lake through the back windows. Feeling safe and cared for was sometimes a scarce commodity. But could she relax when Simon hadn't been found or when Marcus Harper was still out there?

Her phone buzzed. Jasper was all right. Before she could text back, she heard a shout from the back hall.

She pushed out of her seat and went to see what it was, just for the sake of stretching her legs. The receptionist glanced at her, the look on her face very much like *not my problem*. Maybe she was only having a bad day.

Destiny looked through the round window and spotted a desk area with two nurses on one side and treatment rooms on the other. Brent Rammington struggled with Richard, both of them looking haggard.

She headed through the door. "Is everything—"

Brent stepped back and lifted a gun, pointing it at Jasper's father. "It's over, Richard. I won't let you do this."

One of the nurses gasped. Another jabbed her finger at something under the desk. A panic button? There were armed operatives outside, but this one man had slipped in. Destiny reached for her phone to alert them that she was in need of assistance.

Uh-oh. Her phone was still on the chair. She'd set it down when she heard the shout.

She glanced at the nurses but didn't want to ask aloud for them to call the police. "Brent?" When she didn't get his attention, she said louder, "Mr. Rammington?"

He kept his gun pointed at Richard.

Jasper's father said, "Stay back, Destiny. I've got this handled."

"Yeah." Brent sneered. "Like you have everything handled. Right? Well, no more. I won't let you destroy me."

"Neither of us had any choice, Brent. We did what we had to do." Richard sounded almost sad and definitely regretful. "I'm as sorry as you are that it turned out this way."

"I don't need your sorry," Brent said. "I'm done, and so are you." He shifted the gun.

Destiny saw the intention in his eyes.

The door behind Brent slammed open. One of the Famous Ones stumbled in, blood running down the side of her face. She looked *mad* as she lifted a gun and fired faster than Destiny could understand what was happening.

Brent's gun went off at the same time.

His body jerked, and he fell. Richard hit the floor. Destiny ducked down behind the counter and covered her ears.

"Clear!" Oh yeah, the Famous One was pissed.

Destiny stood so she could see the operative. "Everything all right?"

"No. I got blood on my favorite shirt."

Destiny asked, "Richard?"

"I'm good. Brent might not make it." His words might have sounded cold but she saw so much grief and disappointment in his eyes it stole her breath.

The operative said, "That's what happens when someone tries to kill one of ours. They die."

She turned and went out the door she had come in, swiping a gauze packet from a storage container on the shelf on her way out.

One of the nurses asked, "Should we still call the police?"

THIRTY-SEVEN

"And then Gage came down because he heard the gunshot." Destiny blew out a breath.

Jasper eased himself into a seat, tugging her over so he could hug her for a second. "You're okay?"

"Yes, and so is your father. He hit his head, so he is getting checked out."

Jasper nodded, his cheek against her forehead. He'd already told her that Blake was fine.

"Are you sure *you* are okay?" She shifted and looked at him.

"I was knocked out for a second, but the EMT checked, and there are no signs of a concussion." The firefighters had pulled the FBI tactical team out of the debris, and he was still thanking God there hadn't been any fatalities. It was a miracle the injuries hadn't been worse than they were.

Jasper could hardly believe it. The whole thing had made him pray, and he hadn't stopped—first thanking God for the safety and health of everyone and then to ask for success and Simon's safe return. "I just want this guy arrested. Enough running around, chasing him. Looking for Simon. I need him in cuffs."

She nodded. "I feel like I'm spinning fifteen plates, trying to keep up with everything. The Famous Ones are in some secret meeting outside."

"I saw that when I came in. I guess they don't like that one of their people was hurt and Brent gained access to the medical center."

"Half of them had gone after a lead. They were spread thin. They aren't invincible, and when I told them that everyone makes mistakes, they did *not* like it." Destiny winced. "I didn't win the argument."

She was cute.

"I'm sure they'll figure it out. Everyone is running on empty, and Brent was taken care of." He felt the burn of tears in his eyes. Not a normal occurrence for him, he didn't like it and had to shift to distract himself with movement.

"I'm sorry. He was family to you."

Jasper cleared his throat. "At least he's stable. The Famous One who shot him didn't hit anything vital, and we should be able to talk to him soon."

She nodded.

He reached over and took Destiny's hand. "And yet he was going to kill my father? That doesn't make him family anymore." His uncle was dead to him. Even though he hadn't been biologically related, that didn't take anything away from the sentiment. "Family takes care of each other. Unless they can't, in which case, the rest pull together to cover that one person."

He wouldn't have said he needed someone to take care of him. His relationship with Tessa had been like that, with him trying to "fix" her problems and heal her trauma for her. With Destiny, it was a whole lot different and far healthier.

She was the kind of woman he'd been looking for, and he'd get the chance to be a father to her baby. He wanted to protect and love them for as long as he could. But there would be times when she would take care of him. When he got sick, or he was injured. Times when their relationship would be an equal partnership.

Lord willing, they would have years of good times.

Gage stepped out from the back and into the waiting area. Jasper and Destiny stood. Gage gave Jasper a back-slapping hug, then kissed Destiny's cheek. "Brent is stable, and the doctor gave us the green light to question him."

A uniformed officer stood at the door. As they entered, Romeo Alvarez held out his hand. "You good, bro?"

"Thankfully, everyone is."

Romeo gave him an odd look but said nothing. Jasper tucked Destiny by the corner in Brent's room, dragging over a chair for her to sit. He didn't want her within arm's reach of the guy. She seemed grateful for the chair.

Jasper and Gage faced Brent, standing at the end of the bed. Brent wore a hospital gown, and his face was pale. The bandage must be under the clothing, under where he'd been tucked in with blankets. His arms were free of the covers because they were both cuffed to the bed rails.

This man, whom he had considered family, wouldn't even look at him. "Explain it to me because I'm trying to understand, but I need your help."

Brent said, "It's between me and your father."

"And Marcus Harper." Jasper hadn't met the older African American man more than a couple of times. It was shocking to believe that he was the kingpin, a man who had bombed a container ship in Tacoma so many years ago. A man who'd destroyed so many lives, let Jamal Reed take the fall for it, and then hired Malik Henderson to make yet more bombs so he could control Benson. So he could sweep up more territory every month.

Jasper asked, "Where is Simon Olson?"

Brent said nothing, but the look on his face didn't spell anything good. "When he takes someone, they don't come back."

"Then tell me where to find him." Jasper shrugged. "I don't need your opinion. I just need the relevant information to get my friend back." He slapped his chest, which hurt a lot, thanks to the bruise. "So talk."

Brent looked at Destiny, then around the room. Looking for something to focus on while his mind tried to come up with an answer.

Which meant it would probably be a lie.

Gage took a step closer. "You're in serious trouble, but you can cooperate. That's all the leverage someone like you has. After all, what do you think will happen when you're accused of the attempted murder of a state senator? Not gonna go good for you."

Gage used his blue-collar background as a tactic in the same way Jasper used the way he'd grown up to connect with guys in cuffs like Brent. Business leaders and people with money had to face the same justice as everyone else.

Gage continued, "You know how to contact him. The way you know a whole lot about what he's been doing."

"You go after him, you'll all die. That's what you found out at the church, right?"

No, that meant the kingpin considered them a threat. Marcus Harper felt the need to take out as many cops as possible to prove his power.

Jasper asked, "Why do you think we want to find him? To stop this from happening."

"And he took one of your people."

"What will he do?"

Brent said, "Nothing good. He's making it personal, which means you're gonna regret it. Plus, he's got that computer guy from Vanguard, so he can put a dent in their operation."

"So, destroying them is still the goal?"

"In war, you go after the low-hanging fruit first. Then the bigger threat, after you've seen what they are capable of."

Brent was nothing like the man he'd known for years. Was this his true face?

Jasper fought back the frustration that he or his father had been duped. "Have fun in prison. I'm sure it'll be just like the spa."

Brent's face twisted.

"We'll have to make sure Marcus Harper ends up in the same cell block. Since you're friends." He turned away and motioned with a tip of his head for Destiny.

She had already stood and gone out the door first.

"What is it?" From her hard expression, there was an update.

She said, "The list of vehicles registered to that shell company was long, too long to track them all down. But we didn't have to. They have GPS, and most of them are located in a parking lot at a manufacturing plant that the Northwest Counter-Terrorism Taskforce is now very interested in."

"This come from Peter?"

Gage stepped out of the room and shut the door. Officer Alvarez leaned over, listening intently.

Destiny said, "He got all of this from Simon's computer. Anyway, there are three vehicles currently on the road. The Famous Ones are accompanying any Vanguard operative who wants to join, and they're going to pull over those cars."

"That's the police's job."

Gage nodded—but what was the lieutenant agreeing to?

"Vanguard wants Simon back," Destiny said. "If there's an arrest, we will ensure the police are on scene."

"Or we could just head out now." Jasper folded his arms and glanced at Gage. "Do you do this with Clare?"

The lieutenant chuckled. "Yes. And I want Simon back as much as Vanguard, so on this one, I'd get the information and probably give them a head start. The responding units can be a minute or two behind, but that's all."

"So you're not mad?" Destiny glanced between them. "Peter figured you'd be mad, but he is just worried about Simon."

"We all are." Jasper touched her shoulder. "Give me the information."

THIRTY-EIGHT

"I don't like it, but I also don't want to leave you here." Jasper stepped outside first, glancing around like she'd seen the Famous Ones do so many times. Situational awareness, they'd called it.

"I don't want you to leave, either. So, it makes sense to go. All we're gonna do is watch from the safety of the car."

He motioned left. "I parked over there."

Destiny said, "They want us to take *that* car." She pointed to an SUV at the curb. "Keys are under the floor mat. Allyson gave me the door lock code."

Jasper frowned. "Looks like an armored federal SUV."

"Good. Then you won't need to worry about me being in it."

As far as she could see, she would be safer with Jasper. The Famous Ones had been messaging since they left. Asking if she was all right, telling them that Penny was fine, even with the bump on her head, and then asking again if she was all right. They had Peter with them, and the whole group had rolled heavy to the SUV they'd ascertained was the one.

The police were being given the information for the other two.

Destiny hadn't exactly lied, but the Vanguard staff had been creative with what they sent over and who needed to know what.

Jasper pulled out of the parking lot. "This thing is like driving a tank." He motioned to the screen. "Put the location in."

"Actually, it should come up with the GPS tag on the vehicle we're headed for as well as how to get there. So, it'll direct you to them even if they're moving."

"Fancy."

Destiny said, "I had no idea half of this stuff existed. I mean, why would a waitress have a clue about the tech they use?"

"If you decide you don't want to work for Clare, you can be whoever you want. Have your baby and go back to school."

"I need to support myself."

"I get that," Jasper said. "What I'm saying is that it's not a hard line. You could be a waitress again if you want. I heard Vanguard has a cafeteria."

Destiny gasped. "That's a closely guarded secret. But if you ever go, get the cheesecake. It's *amazing*."

Maybe he was only distracting her from thoughts about what'd just happened. Or worry over Simon. Either way, it was working.

Jasper chuckled. "Do they cater weddings?"

"A guy like you is going to have a company cafeteria cater his wedding?" Destiny rolled her eyes. "I'd think you would hire out the fanciest hotel in Benson."

"Or do like Blake and Violet and find a beach, go on vacation, and stretch it to a honeymoon."

She gasped. "They're not!"

"Spring break. But you didn't hear it from me."

"That dirty scoundrel. He said nothing." She was going to smack him upside the back of his head for keeping her out of his wedding plan ideas. Although, maybe not, considering she'd been giving them all the cold shoulder in not wanting to tell them she was pregnant.

She let out a long sigh.

"Anytime. Anywhere. For the record." He reached over and held her hand. "As far as weddings go."

She knew he'd been planning something big with Tessa, though maybe that was why he thought marrying her was right. Because that style wasn't her. It seemed more like what Tessa's mother would've wanted. What had been expected of both of them.

Destiny said, "I like working for Clare. It's been crazy nerve-wracking lately, but maybe that's not normal? And if it gets to be too much, she was talking about putting a daycare in the Vanguard building. Maybe I could run that?"

"Like I said. Do whatever you want." Jasper let go of her hand and drove after the vehicle they were all praying had Simon inside and the kingpin so they could arrest him.

She prayed again. It was all she could do right now. It was up to the Vanguard operatives with their weapons and training and the police to take Marcus Harper down and get Simon back. She had no problem not being in the middle of it, though Jasper would probably rather be there.

"I keep praying for all this. That's all I can do, right?" She glanced at him, but he was focusing on the road. Did he want to talk about this? "My life was so far off trajectory that I had no idea what was happening. My plan and reality diverged, and I was spinning out. And under it all, I knew what to do. I've learned and studied enough that I discovered the foundation that is supposed to be there when things go wrong. God holding me up. Comforting me."

"Do you think He will help my dad and me figure out how to care for my mom?" Jasper turned a corner. "I don't want to put her in the wrong place, but I want to know she's not going to be hurt when my life changes. Soon. When I have a family, and she might not be allowed to be a part of it."

Destiny didn't like excluding someone, but bringing children into a situation where they could be hurt—or they could experience trauma the way Jasper had—wasn't something she was prepared to allow. "This baby is already a miracle in my life. That's how I know I can expect more to come my way."

"I've already found one." He glanced over, and she saw a flash of a smile before he focused again on the road. "Here we go."

Up ahead on the street, two lanes on both sides, traffic had come to a halt. A black SUV was parked sideways across the lanes with the front end in the center turn lane. Someone honked and sped down the hard shoulder to get around the blockade.

Vanguard operatives surrounded the car.

"That doesn't look good."

Jasper squeezed her hand. "But we're going to stay here."

Maybe he felt the need to reassure himself by saying that. She prayed aloud, watching as the Famous Ones approached the SUV. Peter was with them, and a few other operatives. In the distance, she could hear police sirens.

"We need to clear the traffic." Jasper found a button on the dash and flicked it on. Lights flashed from the top of the windshield. "Red and blue. Interesting."

"I have no idea!" Destiny lifted both hands. "Seriously, I don't know why they have those. They aren't police."

"But I am." He laid on the horn and cars parted in front of them.

Destiny held the door handle while checking her phone. "The text thread is silent." Why had she felt the need to say that aloud? "That's how you know they are working." She smiled to herself, and then a message popped in.

The Famous Ones thought she should back off. She relayed it to Jasper. Before she got the words out, Allyson tossed a black canister under the front end of the SUV. It detonated beneath the engine and flipped the vehicle up, over, and onto its roof.

Metal screamed as the SUV hit the ground like a bug flipped onto its back.

Vanguard's Famous Ones surrounded the car, pulling open doors and dragging out the occupants. Multiple people. "There's Simon." Peter had pulled him out.

"Where's Harper?" Jasper jogged his foot, bouncing his knee.

"Don't feel like you have to stay with me if you want to make that arrest. This car is secure, and I'll lock the doors." She gave him a nudge. "Go. Do your job."

Jasper leaned over and kissed her. "I love you."

"I had a feeling." She smiled, feeling mischievous, given how close to being over this was. Eventually they'd have a normal day, right? Or this trend would continue, and they would be in for years of it feeling new between them. Even if life settled, she hoped their relationship would feel new for a long time to come. "And you have to know I've been in love with you since—"

Someone thumped the metal of the SUV's hood.

Jasper's head whipped around at the same second that she looked. Marcus Harper stood at the front end of the SUV with blood running down his face. He lifted a gun.

Light flashed from the front of the muzzle. The bullet impacted the windshield. It splintered in a few circles, barely wider than the bullet. The rest of the windshield remained intact.

"Huh."

Behind Marcus, operatives descended on him, dragging the gun from his hand and shoving his face against the hood. There was a lot of yelling, but Destiny tuned it out.

She turned to Jasper. "What was I saying?"

Humor lit his eyes. "You were saying you love me?"

"Was I?" She tipped her head to the side. "Seems to me like you and I make no sense on paper; we sometimes work for rival organizations, and I live in an impenetrable tower."

"I didn't have a problem getting in."

"That is worrying."

Jasper chuckled. He leaned over. "Enough talking."

His lips nudged hers.

"I do love you."

He said, "I know."

And he kissed her.

THIRTY-NINE

"Good afternoon." Jasper set his phone on the podium. The breeze ruffled his hair, but he ignored the need to press it back down. The suit he wore was one he'd had in his locker, since he'd showered at the precinct. "I'm Detective Jasper Hollingsworth. I have with me Police Commissioner Russ Franklin, Captain Dennis McCauley, and Destiny Reed, who is representing Vanguard Private Security and Investigations."

He didn't look at her, or he'd get distracted all over again by the dress she'd put on, even though she had a blazer over it. Her sisters had shown up at the police department to help her fix her hair. The Famous Ones had been absent since the take-down. They were the "action, please, no paperwork, thanks" kind of operatives the police department would never see eye to eye with.

But he would be forever grateful to them for how they'd saved and protected Destiny.

"Each of us, not just up here but each of you, has been touched personally by the actions of a criminal kingpin who has terrorized Benson for a number of months now. No one has been able to ignore this man's activity, and as a community, we've seen people come together. Groups previously at odds have shaken hands and worked alongside each other."

He glanced around. "Companies that protect us, even when we don't realize they are doing so, have worked tirelessly with the police department, partnering to keep Benson safe. And law enforcement would like to extend our gratitude to Vanguard for their assistance."

Destiny's smile had an edge to it. Probably because he'd said, "assistance." As if he'd give them more credit than that.

Jasper watched Captain McCauley hand Destiny a plaque. They stood beside each other for a photo, and then he went back to the podium.

"Benson's first responder community and our federal agent partners arrested Marcus Harper today, the mastermind behind a container ship bombing in Tacoma two decades ago. More recently, Mr. Harper has proven himself a worthy adversary. But the cause of justice is something we all must answer to. And Mr. Harper's day has come." Jasper looked around at the crowd, realizing how many reporters were recording this with their phones.

He said, "Charges were filed this morning, and the Benson district attorney's office will now be taking the baton from the police department. Mr. Harper will face a judge. The police department and our partners will be working with the DA to ensure justice is served. Thank you all for coming."

He turned away from the podium while the crowd erupted into questions.

The few he heard were about him and Destiny. To answer the question without saying anything, he wrapped his arm around her, and they headed away together. Up the steps into the police department.

He hit the button on the post to be admitted. They

stepped into the lobby and the hallway that separated the PD's ground-floor presence from the FBI satellite office.

None of the people here looked happy. The agents hadn't come out for the press conference and were instead having a group meeting. A picture of the traitorous agent who had been outside Harper's house hung on the whiteboard.

Stella walked to the window and lowered the blinds.

"Well, then."

Jasper squeezed Destiny's shoulders. "I'm sure they'll find him and figure out what's going on."

"I'm just glad Simon is all right."

"Seems to me like there's a whole lot of 'all right' going around." He turned to her, and she slid her arms over his shoulders to lace her fingers around the back of his neck. He said, "My dad. Your brother. Me, you. Clare and Gage and Baby Kara. Peter and Selena. Simon is back at his desk where he wants to be."

She nodded. "It does seem like a lot of 'all right' and more."

"Mmm." He lowered his head and kissed her. This wasn't going to get old anytime soon. There was so much to discover, and their lives would be constantly changing as the baby developed. After she had the baby, they would learn how to parent a child that wasn't conceived under good circumstances. But this child would be God's goodness to them all of his or her life—and they got to be that for the child as well. "Marry me."

Destiny chuckled.

"Is this what I have to look forward to?" Blake's voice came from Jasper's left.

He turned his head, not losing the contact with Destiny, so they had their heads together facing her brother.

Beside Blake, the police commissioner clapped him on

the shoulder. "It's only gonna get worse, kid. Thanksgiving. Birthdays. Baby showers. Births. Toddler birthday parties with clowns and terrible punch. Preteen drama. *Teenage* drama. I haven't decided which of those is worse yet. Driver's licenses. High school graduations." He wandered off, laughing.

Blake eyed them.

"Sorry, bro." Jasper cleared his throat and started to step back from Destiny.

Blake waved a hand. "Don't sweat it. Violet and I just have to get married before Destiny can't fly. So the two of you can be there."

Destiny sucked in a breath. "You really are getting married?"

Blake smiled adoringly at his sister. "She's making an honest man out of me."

Jasper grinned. "Maybe we should make it a double ceremony."

"Get your own idea." Blake mock-punched him. "This one is mine."

Destiny laughed. Jasper watched her brother lean down and kiss her cheek. "Love you, sis."

"Yeah, yeah." Destiny gently pushed him away. "Love you, too."

Blake strolled away down the hall.

"You keep talking about a wedding, but aren't you jumping about fifteen steps?"

Jasper shrugged. "Am I?"

Destiny lifted one hand and started counting off her fingers. "Dating. Meeting my sisters as my boyfriend. Getting engaged. Having our first fight. Making up. Premarital counseling. Which brings me to the whole church thing."

"I'll go with you." It was the next step for him anyway.

"And the rest will come in due time, but fair warning, your hair will be smoking because we'll be going so fast."

"Good, even though it's tacky. But it's tackier for me to be huge when we get married, but everyone will think we did all this out of order and it's your baby." Destiny bit her lip. "Maybe people will just think what they want to think, and we'll have grace from God regardless. We know the truth and where our hearts are."

"Don't worry so much, okay?"

He got the feeling he might spend a lifetime telling her not to worry so much. But it meant she cared. For Vanguard, for their relationship, and for this baby and any others they would have. Worry meant the thing in front of them had weight—and he agreed. These were the most important things.

And he would be there for every second of it to support her.

She touched the buttons on his shirt. "I'm going to worry about you getting hurt. I'm going to worry about how to best raise this child and what people will think. I'm going to worry that what I went through will rear its head again, and I won't be able to control my reaction. I'm going to worry about Violet and Blake and about if your mother is all right. I'll worry how your dad is doing and whether my sisters are getting into trouble. But I promise to ask you to pray with me so I can put the worry aside and trust God with the future and the people we love."

"I promise to be praying already, even before you ask." He realized then he hadn't really stopped since he'd started. There was a lot for him to learn, but he was in exactly the place he needed to be. "But I'll always stop and pray with you when you ask."

"I love you, Jasper Hollingsworth."

"I love you, too."

He kissed her, and the lobby around them erupted into clapping and cheering. When he was good and finished, he lifted his head and saw her smile.

He heard someone say, "Told you," and he looked over.

River stood beside Tessa just inside the door, a dog sitting on either side of them. Tessa had the biggest smile on her face. She burst into laughter, and her dog barked. Then she nodded, gave a loud whoop, and kept the clapping going.

Destiny let out a contented sigh that he caught even with the noise. Jasper liked the sound of it a lot. He took her hand. "How about a tour of the police department?"

She grinned. "Is there a cafeteria?"

He gave her a quick kiss. "I guess you'll have to find out."

FORTY

Two months later.

Destiny heard the distinct sound of a crying baby. She winked at the young woman who sat behind her former desk and knocked gently on Clare's office door.

She heard a muffled "Come in" and entered.

Clare said, "Thank goodness it's you. Is he here?"

"Not yet." Destiny reached for Baby Kara.

"I've got to change my shirt because the lovely Kara just puked on me."

Destiny smiled, even though it wasn't funny. Thankfully, Clare had a full bathroom and several changes of clothes in her office. Destiny walked with the baby across the room, looking at the décor and absently rocking her. It was naptime for the eight-week-old—and nearly for Destiny, too.

While Clare had been navigating life with a newborn, Destiny's unborn child was getting bigger. Rapidly, by the size of her. Destiny's sisters liked to say, "Whoa!" every time she saw them. Then they kissed her belly and Hope always asked if she could read the baby a story.

Usually, they all fell asleep on the couch, waking up when Jasper got home from work at whatever random time that his shift ended. Or his investigation concluded.

They had been married a few weeks. Destiny's role at Vanguard had shifted and would again when the baby was born. She was in the process of setting up the daycare and would manage it after her baby was old enough that he or she could come to work with her.

Jasper had mentioned changing jobs several times but hadn't found anything that suited him yet. His dad had even pitched a partnership, but it would require traveling across the state, and Jasper didn't want to do that. His mother was settled in the Purliss Residential Center, and his father had started a private venture.

Still, she worried that he'd see this as her attempt to get him out of the police department.

It was in the back of her mind constantly that he risked his life on the job. Not that many of the other options for a man with his skills would be less dangerous. But she was worried anytime he worked a shift.

If being a cop was what he wanted to do, then she was going to support him—and ask him to pray for her as she grew and, hopefully, learned how to let go of the worry.

"Knock, knock."

She glanced over and saw him enter, closing the door behind him. His suit and tie and the fresh haircut he'd gotten the day before made her husband look more handsome than Destiny had a right to have ever expected. But yet again, God had given her more than she could've asked for or imagined. The baby she was carrying, the man who loved her. Destiny didn't deserve them any more than she deserved God's grace.

But He was so good, and her life was richer than she ever would've believed it could be.

"Hey, there."

"Hey yourself, handsome." She lifted her face, and he touched his lips to hers.

"Holding a baby looks good on you."

Destiny smiled. "Well, that's a good thing, I guess, all things considering."

"Everything all right?"

"Yes." Had he been worried that this meeting that Clare's assistant had called was about Destiny? She had been to an appointment with him just yesterday, and they'd seen the ultrasound images. The baby was developing right on schedule. "Everything is good."

Clare came out of the bathroom. "Jasper. Thank you for coming. Have a seat."

Destiny carried the baby to the bassinet behind Clare's desk and laid Kara down so she could sleep. Then she took a seat beside her husband. He threaded his fingers between hers.

"As you know, the last few weeks have given me a new perspective," Clare began. "In becoming a mother and speaking with colleagues who are parents. Or about to be." She smiled at them. "I've realized I need to shift my role here at Vanguard. The company is constantly expanding. A number of our teams are currently breaking into multiple smaller teams in order to operate more effectively around the world, and I've set up a new department."

Destiny had been read in on it and the recent acquisition of the Accountant's Office protocol. The whole thing was incredibly complex but boiled down to one thing: Keeping people safe so they could live their lives in peace.

Clare continued, "I would like to take on a role that would

look a lot more like a board member advising the Vanguard CEO but ultimately letting them run the company with the final say as they see fit. Naturally, that CEO would have to be someone I trust. Someone I know I can count on, who has proven time and again that they are a person of high caliber. Someone who puts others above themselves and understands the value of loyalty and family."

Destiny swiped a tear from the corner of her eye. No point kidding herself that they didn't see it. The fact Clare thought that about the man Destiny had married? She closed her eyes for a second. *Thank You.* God had been overwhelmingly good to her. It made her wonder if she'd needed this before things went horribly wrong in her life, but right now, all she had was trust in Him and the joy in this moment.

She rejected the worried thoughts in her mind, taking them captive as the Bible said to, and thanked God again.

Jasper squeezed her hand.

Clare said, "Jasper Hollingsworth, would you like to be the next CEO of Vanguard Private Security and Investigations?"

She heard his intake of breath.

He turned to her. "Destiny?"

She smiled at him. "What do you say?" He had to know it was his decision, not one based on her fear as a factor. "If you want to be a cop or a plumber or a library volunteer, or the Vanguard CEO or the greeter at the grocery store, I know you'll do great. Because it's what *you* want to do. Whatever it is, it's your choice."

He looked at her with a little bit of awe. "I have been thinking lately that I need a change without knowing what it should be."

"Gage and I talked about it at length," Clare said. "He and I believe you'll be a great fit, both because of your family's incredible reputation and because you've made a reputation for yourself in your own right. As a cop and as a good man."

Destiny grinned. "Told you."

Jasper chuckled. "Thank you." He glanced at her, then looked at Clare. "I'm a little amazed you think I have what it takes to take over from you, and I'm happy to hear you'll be staying on as an advisor." He swallowed. "I love the idea. It's perfect."

Destiny let out the breath she'd been holding. Was this what he wanted? The change he'd been looking for, that he said he'd found in her. But he'd still seemed kind of restless and unsatisfied. This could be it.

He had a measured tone when he said, "I'll be close to my family and able to do what I love in a new way."

She bit the inside of her lip. He sounded nervous. She squeezed his hand, just to reassure him in her own way that she had his back. No matter what.

"On a much wider scale." Clare smiled. "Even your father agreed you were meant for something great. Not that being a detective isn't an honorable path. But then he mentioned that this could be a stepping stone to running for governor, so I think I'll leave that one with the two of you."

Jasper groaned. "That man. He only thinks about politics."

Destiny chuckled. "I think you could absolutely be the governor someday. Who knows?" She didn't exactly want to live the life of a politician's wife, but it was up to Jasper.

All she knew was that God would continue to be good, and her life would look nothing like she imagined.

Jasper said, "All right. Let's talk about this. I'm absolutely interested in running Vanguard."

Destiny smiled so wide her cheeks hurt. A couple of stray

tears ran down her face, and Jasper gathered her to his side, kissing her forehead. He whispered, "I'll be your boss."

Destiny gasped. Her heart was full of laughter. "I've signed an NDA. I can't possibly reveal any secrets from before your time. No matter what torture you use, it won't work."

Jasper shifted, and Clare looked at her as well. Amazingly, Destiny hadn't even thought about Africa when she said that. The memories would fade as life moved on. Her child would never know the terrors she had been through.

Jasper would work to make the world a little safer.

So that other women like Destiny, trapped and without hope, would find rescue and family just like she had.

There was nothing she wanted more.

Destiny smiled. "Let's do this."

KEEP READING FOR...

- Where to find more great Lisa Phillips books.

- How to sign up for Lisa's newsletter and get a FREE book.

- Where to find Lisa on social media.

ABOUT THE AUTHOR

Find out more about Lisa Phillips at her website, where you'll discover more romantic suspense fan-favorite series and heart-pounding thriller novels.
https://authorlisaphillips.com/

If you loved this book, please consider sharing about it on social media. Or leave a review at your book retailer website, on Goodreads, or on Bookbub. Your review will help others find great books to entertain and encourage them!

For a FREE novel from Lisa Phillips, scan the QR code below to connect to Lisa's newsletter and be the first to hear about sales, new books, and recommendations for your TBR pile.

Find Lisa on Social Media!

facebook.com/authorlisaphillips

instagram.com/lisaphillipsbks

bookbub.com/authors/lisa-phillips

ALSO BY LISA PHILLIPS

Find out more about Benson First Responders on the series page:

https://authorlisaphillips.com/product-tag/benson-first-responders/

Benson First Responders is a continuation of Last Chance Downrange. Read the whole Last Chance Downrange series now!

Point of Impact

Hard Target

Hollow Point

Terminal Velocity

Audio Available from Podium Publishing

Find more stories based in Last Chance County and Lisa's full backlist at Lisa's website:

https://authorlisaphillips.com/all-books/

Other series by Lisa:

Brand of Justice (Thriller series)

Benson First Responders (Christian Romantic Suspense)

Last Chance Fire & Rescue (Sunrise Publishing)

Chevalier Protection Specialists

Last Chance County

Northwest Counter-Terrorism Taskforce

Double Down

WITSEC Town (Sanctuary)

And numerous other titles including several from

Love Inspired Suspense.

www.ingramcontent.com/pod-product-compliance
Lightning Source LLC
Chambersburg PA
CBHW021150310726

48971CB00002B/572